KELLY LORD

Cover designed by: Tantic Designs
Formatted by: Phoenix Book Designs

Trigger Warnings

Violence, gun violence, criminal acts, mature language, abusive language, mention of sexual assault, degradation, mention of drug use, murder, and bereavement.

CHAPTER ONE

KIERA BLAKE

Blowing the loose tendrils of hair from my grease-dappled forehead, I'm determined to get this engine up and running even if it kills me. I've spent all day on my back beneath this pig of a car. I'm in desperate need of a coffee break. Bodie and I are swamped with work, picking up the slack from when Dad hung up his wrench through ill health. He and our mom moved to the coast, hoping the sea air would help with his emphysema. He can't fix cars with an oxygen tank strapped to his back, poor guy. It killed him to leave, but Mom called us yesterday saying they both love early retirement. Which is good, I guess. The garage is like his third child. It's our family legacy. Our grandpa started Blake Autos here in Mountview back in the early fifties, and we're determined to keep it going strong and hand it down to the next generation. Well, that's the plan. That's if we don't fall victim to all the gang warfare tearing up these parts. Bodie is a member of the Knight Hawks Motorcycle Club, fronted by his childhood bestie and the embodiment of all my dirty fantasies, Jason Knight. Not that he'll ever notice. The fucker still treats me like a kid at twenty-three. I'm only two years younger than he is. To him, I'll always be Bodie's little sister. Jason will never see me as anything else. I'm probably the only person besides his mom who still calls him by his birth name. Nowadays he goes by his nickname, Havoc. That's what his biker buddies call him. The folks around here call them a gang. But they're nothing like the thugs who rode into town last year. Those guys call themselves the Jackals, and like a pack of savage dogs, they've preyed on the good people of Mountview, picking off their businesses one by one.

"Bodie, are you there?" I call out. "I need you to hand me a torque wrench." I hold out my hand, flexing my fingers.

"Just a second," Bodie replies from across the garage. "I'm on the phone."

The sound of a metallic clink near my workstation arouses my suspicion. Someone else is snooping around where they shouldn't be. Using the heels of my work boots, I roll out on my creeper, my eyes bulging as I see who it is.

"Need a hand, Peaches?" Jason asks, using a sweet nickname that means anything but. When we were in school, he said it was because I had a fat ass. It got a laugh out of Bodie, but it gave me a complex. Thanks to him, I wore nothing but Spanx for years. But he was as stunning then as he is now, only broader, sexier. Even his shirts cling to his muscles like they don't want to let go. Jason grins at me, smug as fuck. He's looking down at me, his hair dangling in front of his forehead in dark, messy strands. God, he's handsome, and the arrogant fucker knows it too. Those glinting grey eyes make me wish I could read minds, wondering what the hell he's thinking about. Probably some witty jibe to tease me with. I half expect him to toss the wrench across the garage just to be a dick.

"Not from you," I reply, trying to sound unaffected by him. Not wanting to give him the satisfaction of seeing me squirm. "That's an adjustable spanner, not a torque wrench. I thought bikers could find their way around a toolbox, or is it only your own junk you're familiar with?"

I've insulted him this way plenty of times, insinuating his brains are located far south of his skull. Jason chortles at my comment, then scratches his stubbly chin with his thumbnail, probably thinking of a come-back. I stand and fold my arms beneath my tits, waiting for my chance to retaliate.

"If you weren't Ratchet's sister, a remark like that would've landed you across my lap," Jason mentions, hinting at what he could do if he wanted. "I would have spanked some manners into that peachy ass of yours."

"But you won't because I'm Bodie's little sister?" I scoff at that, using my brother's christened name.

Jason's eyes flare with surprise. "You sound disap-pointed."

Not that I'm inviting Jason to smack my ass. My overalls are padded, but what lies beneath is just a lace thong. And like fuck am I stripping down to that, even if it is my secret kink. Imagine the rush I'd get if I was able to let go. Not with my brother listening. Not with the garage door wide open. But damn, I'm thinking about it. My face is getting hotter, probably looking beet red by this point because my clit likes the sound of that too, and it's growing nice and plump between my labia.

"You wish," I retort.

"Hey, quit ribbing my baby sis and get over here, will you?" Bodie cuts in, keeping his finger over the phone speaker. "You should hear this. It involves you too."

Jason nudges my jaw with his knuckles, grinning like a Cheshire Cat. "Maybe next time, Peaches."

I harrumph loudly. "Mind you don't trip over that ego."

What I say and do and what I fantasize about are two different things. I may be scowling with disgust, but in my head, I've just climbed him like a tree. At least in my head there's no risk of being rejected.

"You're so easy to tease," Jason says to me, his tone softening. He turns around and picks up the torque wrench, then hands it to me, proving he knew what it was all along.

I snatch it from him with an unfriendly snarl. "Get out of my workspace, jerk."

Bodie gawps at Jason impatiently. "Come on, man. This guy won't wait."

"You know, boys might want to fool around with *your* tools if you weren't so hostile." Jason turns away smirking.

"Ahem." Bodie fakes clearing his throat. "Today, please."

I walk a few steps and lean back against my workbench, breathing hard, my heart pounding. Jason always does this. Gets me all riled up, making me attack like a viper. Then when he's gone, the downtime is brutal. Not because of sexual frustration. But because I didn't pluck up the guts to flirt back. Maybe I should have called him out on his bluff and invited him to spank me instead of making fun of it. I've tried dating other guys. It never works out because I keep comparing them to Jason.

Bodie finishes his call, then goes outside with Jason for a smoke. I hear motorcycle engines outside and think nothing of it. I'm used to the Knight Hawks showing up whenever they damn well please like they own the place. But when I crane my head to look, I don't see the Hawks, I see the Jackals.

"Kiera, inside the office, now," Bodie hollers at me, jerking his head. "Don't come out until I say you can."

Doing as he says, I lock the door behind me, then turn the blinds so I can partially see out, but they can't look in. Bodie and Jason stand at the front of the auto shop like guard dogs, not letting any of the redneck fuckers pass the threshold. I strain to listen, deciphering from the mixture of muffled voices as to who's saying what to whom. From the short, disjointed conversation that ends with Bodie telling them to "fuck off", it sounds like he was offered money to pack up and leave town.

"You're gonna regret this." The foreboding last words of the rival biker stay with me after he leaves.

I step out of the office amidst the throaty engine noise and watch them leave in a thick cloud of road dust. Bodie double-takes at me and huffs.

"What did I tell you? Not to come out until I say you can," he berates me.

I fling my hand up at the dusty street. "They're gone now. What did they want?" I ask, expecting him to relay the information.

Bodie and Jason exchange a furtive glance, then Jason mutters that he needs to take a piss, which is charming. Bodie manages a strained smile. "Nothing," he lies, which doesn't alleviate my anxiety. "They came here for tune-ups, but I told them where to stick it. We're not doing business with the likes of them." He reaches up and drags the shutter down.

"We're open until eight," I remind him, frowning bemusedly. "It's only quarter past six."

"Did you remember to eat today?" Bodie asks, sounding like Dad.

I roll my eyes.

"I'll take that as a no then," he says with an exasperated huff. "You can finish up tomorrow. I'll drive you home."

"Where are you going?" I ask suspiciously.

"Nowhere that concerns you," Bodie fires back, shutting me out and treating me like a kid as always.

I can't shake the bad feeling I have that something terrible is about to happen. Bodie drops me home, where I spend three-quarters of an hour scrubbing the stench of fumes and all the oil and grease off me, but even a nail brush and a pumice stone aren't enough to remove the ground in dirt from my work-worn hands. It feels good to be clean again, even if it is only short-lived until tomorrow. With my hair wrapped in a towel, I scour the freezer in nothing but my bathrobe and slippers while looking for something edible for dinner. I pull out a pepperoni pizza, remove the packaging, then shove it into the oven and wait for it to cook. It's not much, but it's enough to settle my hunger so I can at least get some sleep tonight. I'm not sure what time to expect Bodie home, so I lock up the house before going to bed. I'm dog tired, but my thoughts are plagued with worry. Thinking about what those guys said to Bodie and what repercussions we're likely to face. Bodie isn't stupid. I know he's wondering the same thing. Which is why I'm worried about what he and Jason will do. And this brings me back to Jason and what he said to me today. If I were anyone else, he would spank me. God, I want that. Next time, I'll dare him to follow through with it. I play the scenario out in my head, closing my eyes, and letting my fingers glide down my naked body between the warm, soft bed sheets, bringing my knees up slightly and letting them fall to the sides, my stomach tightening as I get closer to my sparsely covered mound. Something I wished I could have done earlier, back when the urge was stronger, stroking my fingers along my shorn pussy lips until my clit grows nice and fat. When I'm satisfied that I've teased myself enough, envisioning Jason's handsome face as he strokes me into a panting mess, I bring my finger up to my open mouth and coat it with saliva. It's easy to mistake my calloused pad for a man's dexterous touch, gliding the slick tip around my swollen nub until I'm seeing stars. I pretend Jason is finishing me with his tongue, lapping at my pulsing clam until it detonates. Then groan through my climax, riding it out with a vigorous rub.

"Oh, Jason," I whimper, my breathing tremulous, the pulse in my clit throbbing as my orgasm wanes.

I don't even pinpoint the moment when I drift off to sleep.

CHAPTER TWO

Bang. Bang. Bang.

B I wake to the sound of incessant knocking on the door. If I didn't know any better, I'd think it was the bailiffs coming to rinse the place for unpaid debts.

"Bodie, can you get that?" I yell groggily, tossing the sheets back.

There's no sign of movement, just the persistent sound of knocking. I fling my robe over me and tie the belt, then shuffle downstairs to answer the door. The cool air hits me square in the face, I scrub the sleep from my eyes and see half of Mountview's police department parked on the roadside at the edge of my lawn. Sheriff Dan Lopez removes his hat, exposing his balding head to the early-morning drizzle, looking at me with those same downturned eyes that he uses whenever he delivers bad news.

"I'm sorry to disturb you at this ungodly hour, Miss Blake. Can I come in?" he asks, clutching his hat against his chest, the golden six-pointed star badge glinting in the light.

"Sure," I reply, opening the door wider. "Is there something wrong?"

Sheriff Dan touches my arm in a comforting gesture. "Inside, hm."

That's when I notice Jason stepping out from behind the two deputies, Carl and Jessa, his eyes puffy and bloodshot, his face drained of color like he's about to be sick.

"What are you doing here?" I instantly bite. "Where's Bodie?"

Jason's watery gaze lingers on me, full of regret, and it doesn't take a genius to work out why they're all here.

"Miss Blake," Dan kindly says, escorting me inside.

My head fills with a foggy cloud of despair as he leads me to the cramped sitting room where most of my parents' stuff is all boxed up ready to be shipped to their beachside cabin. The words "gang shooting" and "dead" ring through my ears like a grenade going off, the shockwaves blasting throughout. Everything else is a blur. The cops leave me sobbing in Jason's arms, hoping and praying this is all one huge mistake. Which doesn't turn out to be the case. Not as the weeks drag by and the severity kicks in. My parents came home long enough to take care of the formalities, then stayed for the funeral. Dad refused to put the auto shop on the market and said it was mine if I wanted it. I'm keeping it all. The garage. The house. My whole life is here. My brother's essence resides in these walls. Leaving Mountview would feel like we've abandoned him. I'll never do it. I'm going to stay and find the bastard who killed him. Jason knows. He saw who pulled the trigger. He claims it was the rival gang's president. Marcus Jackal. But the last I heard, Marcus was pulled in for questioning, and for some reason, he has a solid alibi that doesn't correlate with Jason's story at all. There's a rumor floating around that Jason is responsible. People are making up their minds and filling in the gaps. I'm not sure what to believe. But maybe there's truth in all the whispering. Jason's monthly cash handouts could be an admission of guilt. He keeps checking in on me from time to time, and he and some of his crew members have been keeping the garage afloat in my absence. It's difficult to distinguish the truth from lies after the seed of doubt has been planted. I don't know what to believe. A part of me thinks I will never know the truth. But I owe it to Bodie to find out.

Getting my shit together, I focus my energy on getting justice for Bodie. This includes going through his belongings to see if I can find any signs of a dispute between him and Jason, which unsurprisingly, there aren't. They were as tight as brothers. Nothing else makes any sense. Just because Sheriff Dan is dating Jason's mom, it wouldn't be enough reason to keep his ass out of jail. If he thought Jason was guilty, he would have acted on it. Dan is like Judge Dredd around here. He is the law. All I find is an old matchbox in his overall pocket from a seedy dive bar called the Rusty Chain, which is where the Knight Hawks go to blow off steam. I've heard them talking about it, and it's not somewhere I personally want to go through the fear of contracting hepatitis. Bodie will blow a gasket from beyond the grave when he sees what I'm about to do. I try not to think about it as I dress in the skankiest outfit I can find in my closet. I don't own much, but my thrift store bargains enable me to pull off a slutty rocker look. The plan is to blend in with the regulars, not stick out like a sore dick. My tight stonewashed jeans that are slashed front and back, strappy red, low-cut top, and matching red heels make me feel somewhat feminine. I finish the look by blow-drying my hair into loose waves, adding some provocative makeup, and squirting on way too much perfume, and now I'm good to go.

A lone biker crawls past the house on an old cruiser with tall handlebars. Whoever it is rides past the house every day. I can't see his face through the visor, but the fact that he's keeping tabs on me sets off warning bells in my head. Thankfully, he fucks off before my cab arrives.

I grab my purse and phone, then take the cab to the Rusty Chain. It's only a ten-minute car ride from my house, but it's amazing how fast the scenery changes on the far side of town. Mom always says it's where all the riffraff comes from, which is funny because Jason grew up here. Obviously, she made excuses for him. Saying he's just a good kid who was born on the wrong side of the tracks, but that remains to be seen. So, here I am, standing on the wrong side of all that's decent, honest, and good, questioning my choices as I step out onto the dusty parking lot, casting a critical eye at my surroundings. This place is everything Bodie warned me about. He said if I ever stepped foot in a place like this, he'd slap me with a bible and toss me into the nearest convent. He was only half-joking, but really, I can see why he wouldn't want me anywhere near this hellhole. The Rusty Chain is a rundown shack that ought to be bulldozed to the ground. The barred windows remind me of the jailhouse downtown, and the tin roof has more patches than my grandmother's memory blanket. Several greasy bikers check me out from the roadside, so I don't linger any longer than necessary. One of them whistles obnoxiously, so I head inside, passing the bouncer who checks out my tits rather than challenging me for ID.

Weaving between the sweaty bodies in the over-capacitated shack, I make my way to the bar. A band is playing on the tiny stage. The black pitted walls have more craters than the moon. The guy growling down the microphone like he's demonically possessed looks like he's about to swallow it. There's nothing wrong with rock music so long as you can croon along to it. If I try singing along to this, I'll get a sore throat. The drummer might as well be having an epileptic fit as he bangs on the drums, and the guitarists assault the guitar strings like they're scrubbing the stains from their pot-burned muscle tops, their ratty hair flying at all angles. This isn't my scene. I prefer the clubs in town where they play upbeat tracks I can dance to. But here, people are copying the band's moves like a bunch of nodding dogs, their boots and heels shuffling through all the smashed glass on the grimy dance floor. I look around shocked to see a girl on her knees, her head bobbing above a leather-clad biker's groin, her red curls wound tightly around his fingers as he skull-fucks her face. *Nice. Could have at least taken her outside to the back of a dumpster.* Nearby, another couple are frantically banging against the wall, her legs wrapped around the guy's waist, and his jeans slack around his bouncing ass cheeks. *I can't believe my brother used to hang out here.* The game area isn't any better, with a fully naked woman sprawled on her back across the pool table taking three guys at once—one making a meal on her pussy, and the other two sucking beer off her tits. She's clutching fistfuls of cash like she's charging by the second. I'm not easily shocked, but today I've seen everything, and I'm speechless. *What a shithole.* The humid air smells of fifty percent body odor—the smell of sex included—forty percent tobacco smoke, and only ten percent beer. I'm reconsidering my decision to come here, not wanting my face to end up on next week's milk cartons. But it's too late to back out now. I was prepared to suck a dick or two in exchange for information, but judging by all the unwashed miscreants here at the Rusty Chain, I think I'll pass. It'll take more than a few drinks to make these guys look pretty. I'm craving hard liquor. Something to take the edge off my nerves and quell my revulsion. So, I squeeze through the hulking guys at the bar and wave at the barmaid, hoping to catch her attention, but the rocker chick looks right over my head at whoever just pushed in behind me.

"Hey," I complain, turning around to chew the line-hopper out, my words getting snagged in my throat as I lock eyes with Jason.

The expression must melt off my face and morph into a look of pure shock.

"Peaches," he acknowledges me with a suspicious scowl. "What the fuck are you playing at, coming to a place like this and wearing something like that?" His fist clenches as he talks like he's fighting the urge to grab me and drag me out of here kicking and screaming.

I've seen Jason in his kutte plenty of times, but not when he's pissed off at me. Acting all protective and shit. There's just something about a big, strong man, muscled to fuck and inked from the neck down that really does it for me. Especially one who's glaring down at me like he wants to punish me in all ways sinful. It makes me want to conform to his wily ways and bow down to suck his dick the second he snaps his fingers.

"Keira." Jason uses my name to snap me out of my

fantasy. "I'm not kidding. You shouldn't have come here. It's too dangerous."

I recognize some of the Knight Hawks here in the bar. They seem anxious about something or other; I'm not sure why. Then a burly fucker with a scarred face and a mohawk glares at me as if he's looking straight through me. He snaps his gaze at Jason, his steely eyes narrowing with contempt.

"Are you trying to set me up, Hawke? Is this what it is? A setup?" he threatens Jason, getting all up in his face like he's about to start a fight.

Jason doesn't flinch. Not even so much as flicker his eyelids as he holds up his palm to warn off his crew.

"Easy, boys. There's been a misunderstanding," Jason mentions, his voice calm and controlled. "I just need to have a stern chat with my woman, then we can get right back to business."

His woman?

The intimidating Mohawk Guy glares at me, and I clutch onto my purse strap and shrink behind Jason.

"Look at him. Can't even keep a leash on his bitch. What's that say about the rest of his crew?" Mohawk Guy sneers.

That comment almost sparks a reaction from Jason, and I can tell by how his eyes darken and the way his teeth curl over his upper lip in a lethal snarl.

"This is our turf, mutt. Just remember that before you keep running your mouth. My pal, Tex, is a butcher by trade. He'll cut your tongue out and add it to his collection." Jason motions to Tex who rolls his bulky shoulders and cracks his knuckles.

Mohawk Guy skulks off to sit with his pals, then glares at us as he sips his beer. Jason steers me back to the bar, then beckons the bartender over to serve him.

"My usual please, Maxine, and whatever Peaches is having," Jason says to her.

"I'll have whatever he's having," I answer, noticing her smirk as she reaches for the strongest whisky on the shelf.

Maxine pours two glasses, then slides them over to us, her finger brushing flirtatiously against Jason's index, which he blatantly ignores. He leans down to whisper something to me, moving my hair off my shoulders.

"Can you at least try to play along? I'm trying to save your peachy little ass from getting torn apart," he rasps waspishly.

Curling my fingers around the cool glass, I flick my eyes at him, playing my best hand at seduction. "I thought you said I had a great big juicy peach and you wanted to bite it," I retort, puckering my lips in a sarcastic air kiss.

Jason's eyes flare with annoyance. "Careful, Keira. We're being watched."

"I've only come here for answers," I retaliate, looking him dead in the eye. "Maybe Mohawk Guy knows who shot my brother."

Jason grimaces angrily, holding his hand in front of my face to silence me. "Seriously, Keira. You need to shut your mouth." He pinches my lips together to clamp them shut.

Jerking my head back offendedly, I narrow my eyes. "Or maybe you're the one who did it." I knock back my liquor, then slam the glass on the bar.

"I've just about had it with you," Jason growls through his gritted teeth. "Do yourself a favor and go home."

"No," I snap back, snatching his glass and tossing the contents into his face. "You don't get to tell me what to do."

It's just my luck that the band chooses this precise moment to take a break, meaning everyone in the room just heard me yelling. Jason snatches my wrist and holds it tight, sending a stab of panic straight through me.

"Bad move, Spitfire," Jason growls, wiping his face with his free hand.

My blood rushes to my feet, weighing them down.

It suddenly dawns on me how much trouble I'm in. My hunch was right. Bodie's killer has been right under my nose all along. In a fight or flight movement, my free hand flies up to slap Jason hard across his face. Everybody's looking. Even Mohawk Man and his toothless goons. Even Maxine, the skanky barmaid, is gawping at us with her mouth agape. Shocked that someone like me had dared to stand up to the mighty Havoc. There are slack jaws all around. One guy's cigarette is stuck to his bottom lip and is just hanging there, the white smoke unfurling around his face in curled wisps. Jason's face twists with fury, his hands plucking at my flailing arms as I struggle to avoid capture.

Mohawk Man stands up from his chair to get a better view. "Looks like you're losing your touch, Havoc," he calls out to Jason, much to the fury of the Knight Hawks.

"Are you just gonna stand there and let her talk to you that way?" Tex growls. "She ought to be punished – club rules," the buzz-cut tattooed giant not so kindly points out, jabbing his sausage-sized finger at me.

"I'm aware of the fucking rules, Tex. I made them," Jason snarls at him. "Hold the fort while I spank some manners into her. Keep your eye on those fuckers in case the Jackal shows."

"We gotta see proof of her punishment," another guy yells, but I don't see who. "Or else it's time for a change of management."

Jason huffs a curse word under his breath. "Sorry, Peaches. I warned you, but I can't let this one slide," he asserts, grabbing me.

"Get your hands off me!" I wail at the top of my lungs, causing a scene. "You murdering, lying son of a bitch!"

CHAPTER THREE

Jason drags me through the dive bar, my heels scraping across the grimy floor as he pulls me into a dingy room adjacent to the bar. It's not a bathroom, just a dark room with a desk covered with papers. He slams the door and shoves me roughly against the pitted wood, clamping his hand over my mouth. His hands are clean as a biker's hands can be, I guess, but I can still smell a hint of engine oil and nicotine.

"Do you remember me telling you that one of these days your motormouth is gonna land you in trouble?" he growls, and his words hold so much vehemence I'm not sure if it's a warning or a personal threat.

I nod my head, tears pricking behind my eyes.

"Congratulations, you succeeded in pissing me off. What the fuck were you thinking, coming to a biker bar and throwing around wild accusations like that? I can't let you walk out of here without a reprimand; you'll be fucked seven ways from Sunday before you make it to the parking lot. And then what? Who do you think will save your ass after you've discredited me? Tex? Hustle? Rooster?" He huffs a doubtful laugh. "You'll be lucky if they recover your body after the shit you just pulled. If I don't smack some manners into you, people will think I've gone soft, bending the rules for a loudmouth chick just because I'm sweet on her."

The slight admission drains from my mind, making me doubt whether he said it at all. There's no way in hell Jason Knight has any feelings for me. Just guilt for what he did. That's all there is to it.

"It'll make me look weak in front of the club. Do you know how many guys are waiting in the wings to fucking challenge me? Do you?" He huffs, his eyes wild with outrage. "You're a walking liability, coming here, thinking you know shit when you don't know jack. You're not gonna like what happens next, but tough. I gave Bodie my word that I'd look out for you, which leaves me no choice but to stake my claim on you before any of those fuckers out there do it first. And you better believe it, they will. I would if I were on the other side of that door. I'd beat the fucker down to get my hands on you."

I can scarcely breathe, thinking these are my last moments on Earth. Jason's intense glare bores through my eyes, making me realize how much shit I'm in. *Claim me*. I'm not sure what the fuck that means, but I get the feeling I'm about to find out.

"Nod, if you understand me," he orders, and I obey, nodding quickly. "Good, now I'm gonna remove my hand, and you're gonna keep that motormouth of yours shut until I say you can speak."

Jason moves his hand away, and my fingertips feel around blindly for the doorknob. I seize the opportunity to yank the door open, but I'm not fast enough. An inch is all I manage before the fucker is on me in a millisecond, slamming it shut again. This time, shoving my face against the wood. Jason's hard body is flush against my back, sandwiching me between the cold, painted wood and his hard, masculine heat. With a little effort, he pins both my wrists high above my head with one hand, squeezing a little harder than necessary.

"You're either brave or just plain stupid, but you're damn well gonna learn how things work around here. This isn't a day at Disney World, Kiera. Out there, you'll find a bar full of the nastiest fuckers you'll ever meet, just waiting to tear into a peach like you. Now, do yourself a favor and listen to me because I won't repeat it. Do as I say, and I *will* protect you. Disobey me, and you will be severely punished," he rasps against my ear, the gruff rumble of his voice tickling my spine, his hot breath and cologne drowning my senses.

"Let me go," I utter meekly, trembling from head to toe.

"Not so confident now, are you?" he taunts me. "A word to the wise, Princess. If you can't handle a little heat, quit playing with fire, or else you're gonna get burned." Jason nips my ear with his teeth. "Leave what you think you know at the door. It'll do no good carrying the weight of it around with you. Bodie died doing club business. It's my job to avenge him. Not yours. Your cute peach belongs indoors, either beneath the hood of a car or sprawled under me. Pick one, because I prefer both. You're mine, Keira. I've had my eye on you for a long, long time."

I swallow hard, unable to pull free or avoid the solid lump he keeps pressing against my ass. All the back and forth. Every snarky exchange. Jason kept coming back for more like he couldn't get enough. And all this time, it's because he likes me.

"Look," I start, dragging my tongue across my bottom lip. "I just want answers, that's all. If you have any respect for me at all, you'll tell me what really happened."

"Respect?" Jason mutters, releasing a breathy chuckle. "That works both ways. I'll respect you if you respect me."

Jason releases my wrists, sliding his hands around my hips, squeezing almost intimately like a lover. Then he feels around the swell of my breasts, cupping one in his palm, his thumb grazing across the puckered nub of my nipple.

"Is that really fucking necessary?" I utter, my breath skittering through my lips. "This is not the way to earn my respect, just so we're clear."

"You're mine now," Jason mentions, trailing his fingers down my stomach, plucking the button of my jeans open, and sweeping his fingertips across the hem of my panty line, my knees wobbling unsteadily. "It's up to me whether to keep you safe or to toss you out there to the wolves."

I gulp hard as he runs one finger down my lace-covered mound and strokes close enough for him to feel my heat. I don't move a muscle. Frozen to the core. He's a millimeter away from my clenching pussy, no doubt feeling the slickness he's conjuring as he strokes me.

"Why are you doing this?" I ask, my voice straining.

Jason's hot breath gusts against my ear, teeth grazing my earlobe. "To find out for sure that the feelings between us are mutual."

Biting my lip, I stifle a moan as the pad of his finger teases the edge of the lace, wishing he would delve inside. It's too damned hot and cramped in here to be fooling around like this. A trickle of sweat rolls from my hairline and down the side of my temple.

"You wish," I reply, pushing his buttons.

"If they weren't, you'd be telling me to stop," Jason mentions, raising a fair point. "Is that what you want, Peaches? Do you want me to stop?"

I snatch a ragged breath. "No," I admit, my cheeks blazing with heat.

"Didn't think so. But you doubted me," Jason gruffs, his tone lethal as he slides his finger and thumb beneath the elastic of my thong, stroking at first, teasing his way inside, and then plunging between my folds, taking my clit hostage with a light pinch. "You still doubt me even though you're dripping wet."

"Screw you, asshole," I reply without thinking, my sharp tongue getting me deeper into trouble. I like his dominance more than I should, my traitorous pussy creaming at the contact. "If you're gonna spank me, just spank me already."

Jason chuckles, and it's the dark kind that hints at brutal savagery. "Careful, Peaches. Your caustic mouth is making my dick twitch. If you're lucky, you'll get to leave here with a limp and a smile. Keep pissing me off and you'll have difficulty sitting for the next week." He screws his finger deep inside my wet heat and wriggles it around. The gentle stretch feels amazing, not that I'll tell him that. I fight the urge to moan, chewing my bottom lip as he works, but then he starts thumbing my clit with slick dexterity, and I'm done. My eyes roll into the back of my skull, electricity crackling through the bundle of nerves. I try to stop the moans from tumbling from my mouth, but it's no use. I'm not in control here. Jason is, and I rest my head back against his shoulder and enjoy it.

"That's it," Jason coos into my ear. "Let me take care of all that stress."

"It's gonna take more than that," I say, meeting his gaze.

Jason exhales with a breathy chuckle. "Oh, don't you worry about that, sweetheart. You'll be taking a lot more from me by the end of tonight. And if you insist on running that mouth of yours, I know the best way to plug it."

"And you can go fuck yourself," I say defiantly, seeing stars as his skilled fingers dance around my pussy like he's playing an instrument.

I shudder through my climax, my palms pressing flat against the door, feeling the warm trickle of juices running down my thighs. Jason adds another finger, swirling those dexterous digits around the creamy puddle he's created, then he pulls them out and presents them at my lips for me to suck clean.

"Taste yourself," he encourages, his tone dripping with sin. I part my lips, and he stuffs his fingers inside, and I taste my sweet, tangy juices on Jason's warm, salty skin.

"Juicer than a peach," he says, turning me around to hold my jaw, angling my face to his. "How about you give me some of that sugar and see if you really do taste like peaches?" Jason dips down to capture my lips in a searing kiss, controlling the movements, and determining the speed and pressure. It's perfect. Enough to melt my insides and leave me gasping. His fervent tongue boasts the tricks he's learned when eating pussy, and the contrast of his cashmere lips versus his rough stubble stamps its branding mark on me, leaving me flushed and desperate for more.

"You're perfect just as you are, Kiera. I wouldn't change a single thing about you, for what it's worth," Havoc tells me, and it sounds like he means it. "But the wolves are out there hungering for your blood, and I'm not one to share. So, here's how it's gonna be. You're gonna take your punishment like a good girl, and then we're gonna parade your spanked ass around the club for all to see."

My legs shake and wobble unsteadily as Jason drags my jeans and panties down my damp thighs, then steps on them, bunching them around my ankles. He growls with annoyance as he's forced to remove my shoes, and then finishes yanking off my jeans, leaving me standing here bare-assed.

"Bend over the desk and angle that fine peach up for me," he commands me, his voice stern and full of authority. "If you try to use your hands to cover yourself, I'll be forced to tie them down."

I do as he says, too aroused to refuse, and shaking all over. I should feel humiliated and violated, but I don't. It feels good to relinquish control and hand it to someone who's making me feel this good. I trust that he'll keep his word. If not to me, then to Bodie. Obey Jason, and he'll help me. Refuse him, and I don't want to think about the consequences. Maybe he'll throw me to the wolves as he mentioned. But somehow, I doubt it. Something tells me that beneath his tough exterior, there's a decent guy buried deep down in there somewhere. I bend over the desk, move aside a stack of papers, and rest my elbows against the scuffed woodwork. Jason slaps my ass lightly as if to watch how it wobbles. He does this several times on either side. The first couple of slaps feels good, but then he applies more force, and it soon starts to sting. As the swats get harder, the impact sparks fire across my skin. I hear Jason spitting into his palm, and then another five-fingered blaze scorches the opposite cheek. Again, and again, it burns. The tears fall from my glazed eyes, and the sobs skitter through my lips until all I see is a thick white misty fog. All the pain, the tension, the helplessness, and the sheer frustration that I've been feeling all start to melt away with the final few smacks. It leaves me feeling cleansed and revitalized. The veil lifts, and the hot tears feel like they've purified my soul.

"Had enough?" Jason asks, his tone firm, but I detect some underlying remorse there too.

"Yes," I sob, unable to take another swat.

He grabs both sides of my glowing ass. "Do you accept my claim on you?"

"I guess," I reply with a sniff.

Jason presses his fingers harder, dragging a painful squeal from my lips. "Not good enough. Try again. Do. You. Accept. My. Claim. On. You?"

"Yes, yes," I reply, both because it's what I've always wanted, and fuck, because my butt stings like a son of a bitch. "I'll be good, I promise."

"You better," he replies, letting go and stepping back. "In that case, put your panties back on but not the jeans. We're leaving, and I'm afraid you've got to do the walk of atonement to prove you took your punishment."

I'm slightly disappointed by this as I was hoping it would lead to a happy ending.

Guess not.

I turn in time to see him scrubbing the contrite look off his face, and our eyes meet. Sadness versus guilt. I need answers, and he has them. He's looking for redemption, and I'm pretty sure I'm it. If he saves me, he's fulfilling a brotherly oath to Bodie. But that must mean I'm in deeper shit than he's letting on, and by coming here, I've knocked down the first domino. There's no way to stop each one from falling. Not now the floodgates are open. After pulling on my shoes, I snatch up my jeans and purse, wiping my snotty nose on the back of my hand. I'm a sniveling mess, and it pains me to walk through the dingy dive bar with all those beady eyes watching me. Jason claims he must prove I've taken my punishment, but the way some of the guys are looking at me as I walk out of the room holding Jason's arm, I'd say it's more than that. It's like I'm fresh meat. But thanks to Jason, parading me around like a show horse, it means my pussy is off the menu. I'm his. And now everyone here knows it.

"You can thank me properly when we get home," Jason utters into my ear suggestively.

Mohawk Man topples his chair over as he stands, and all his goons follow. They don't seem happy with how things have worked out. But I get the feeling they came here looking for a fight no matter the outcome.

"Gonna need my arm back for a sec," Jason says, shoving me at his pal, Rooster. "Hold on to my girl while I take out the trash."

Mohawk Man pulls out a flick knife.

"Jason!" I gasp with horror.

Jason moves fast, grabbing Mohawk Man's arm, twisting his wrist, then headbutts him smack in the face. Rooster drags me out of the way as Tex and Hustle jump into the fight, throwing punches at the unwelcome guests. Jason shakes the blood from his knuckles, then swoops me up onto his shoulder like a caveman. The unexpected, speedy motion makes me dizzy, the floor bouncing in and out of focus.

"Scream my name all you want when we're fucking. But in front of everyone else, the name's Havoc," Jason remarks, landing another stinging slap on my butt.

CHAPTER FOUR

Jason carries me outside, away from all the hurtling bottles, swinging fists, and all the utter carnage that comes with a biker bar fight. I've never seen anything like it – what I can see from my upside-down angle. It's both scary as fuck and the most exciting thing to ever happen to me. Jason puts me down, and the door swings shut on all the chaos taking place inside.

"Where are you taking me?" I demand as I remove my shoes to pull my jeans back on in the parking lot, the grit and stones biting into the soles of my bare feet.

"The Clubhouse," Jason tells me, being vague with the details.

"Wait, this isn't it?" I thumb behind me.

Jason eyes me sharply. "No, this ain't it," he replies, sounding offended by that.

"Oh, I just assumed," I say before Jason cuts me off.

"You assumed we'd all bundle together under one big blanket and have a gangbang?" He casts a critical eye over me as I button up my fly. "Sometimes I wish Bodie had been more open with you about things. We're nothing like those meatheads in there. We have standards, Keira. The boys and I fixed up a place down by the river. It's not much, but it's clean. It's warm. And it's home." His eyes cut to the bar door as something slams against it. "Let's get you out of here before the shitshow erupts onto the parking lot."

Mohawk Guy comes hurtling through the door, followed by Tex, who strolls out dusting his palms. Hustle and Rooster give his goons a helping hand by tossing them onto the dusty ground.

"Go back and tell your boss I said no. And if he or any of you ever show your faces here again, it won't end well for any of you," Jason warns them.

Mohawk Guy spits blood onto the ground, then glowers at Jason as he gets up. "You're gonna regret this."

Jason pulls out a gun from the waistband of his

jeans. "You've got some nerve, threatening me on my turf." He takes off the safety, and my mouth runs dry.

"Jason, what are you doing?" I murmur, my heart pounding as I curl my hand around his arm.

Jason jerks his elbow away, his face twisting into an angry snarl. "You've got until I count to three to fuck off back to whatever rat hole you crawled out from before I start shooting."

The goons scramble away before Mohawk Guy does. He starts running the moment Jason starts counting. Jason doesn't even get to three; he chuckles after counting to two, watching them scuttle out of view like a cluster of roaches. He puts the safety on, then thrusts the gun back inside the waistband of his jeans, his face stern as he looks at me.

"Never question me in front of the enemy." Jason grabs my wrist and pulls me along. "And you used my real name when I specifically told you not to."

"Uh-oh," Rooster chortles behind me. "Someone just earned another ass whooping."

I hear the guys laughing behind us, their voices fading as I run to match Jason's hurried pace. His hostile body language is making me nervous. I don't want him to be mad at me. I like him better when he's nice. It didn't matter how bitchy I was to him before today. He always shrugged it off. But now it's like the slightest roll of my eyes, angry exhale, or the tiniest little comment is going to earn me a smacked backside or worse. I'm his now, and it's like he's setting an example. If he can't control me, then he can't control anything. And I totally get it. But I get a kick out of winding him up. What the hell am I gonna do for fun now?

Jason leads me to his Harley Davidson cruiser. It's large and sexy, just like him, and he stares at me as if he's expecting me to just get on the back and ride pillion with him. I'm not afraid of bikes. I just don't trust the fuckers who ride them.

"Are you nuts? I'm not getting on that thing with you," I tell him straight. "I'll get cut to bits if I fall off."

Jason gets on the bike and then taps the seat with a smirk on his face. "If you don't, I'll spank you in front of the whole fucking club. How about that?"

Reluctantly, I do as he says, climbing on and wrapping my arms around his toned stomach.

Then I hold on tightly as he kicks off and leaves the guys behind us in a cloud of gritty road dust, the barren scenery whizzing past my eyes in a speedy blur. He takes me through town, turning off down a side road. I assume it belongs to a steelwork company, or at least it did before they abandoned the site. Jason, or Havoc as he asked me to call him, stops outside some rusty gates and then drags them to one side. It's ominous as fuck. There's nothing but overgrown weeds and long grass as far as the eye can see. But then I hear a loud bark, and a huge black Rottweiler comes bounding over to us and darts out through the open gate. Jason stoops down to stroke him, and the dog rolls onto his back to let Jason tickle his belly. The rumble of bikes fills the air as the guys ride past us and leave us standing here beside the open gate.

"Hey there, Dude," Jason greets the dog, rubbing his smooth, short fur and scratching behind his ears. "Did you miss me? I brought someone here to meet you." He turns to me and jerks his head toward the dog. "Bodie and I rescued him when he was just a pup. Didn't have a single tooth in his head. Reckoned he must've been around four weeks old. He was inside a mailbag by the river. Someone tried to toss him in but missed. Sick fucker. It was a stroke of luck we found him – heard him whimpering, and looked inside the bag, and there he was. We hand-reared him, taking turns feeding him every few hours. Fuckin' slept at my side for weeks until he learned to settle alone. He takes up most of my bed; I'm lucky if he'll give me an inch of room."

I flash a wicked grin. "Oh yeah?" I walk over to the dog to pet him, surprised he lets me. He's so friendly, licking out at my hand as I pet him. "Not much of a guard dog, huh? More of a cock block, am I right?" I say, hearing Jason snort in agreement.

"You're honored he's letting you do that," Jason tells me. "The last stranger who tried to pet him, Dude almost took his hand clean off. He must be able to smell Bodie on you."

Jason and I exchange a fond smile at the mention of Bodie's name. It's a tender moment, and my heart clenches a little, the pain bringing a lump to my throat. Not wanting to get all teary-eyed, I sniff and deflect the conversation.

"Wait, what? You named the dog Dude?" I ask, scrunching my face, thinking maybe *dude* was a cute term of endearment. "Couldn't you think of an actual name? It's almost worse than calling him Dog. I thought with him being a biker's dog, you'd pick a cool name like Fang or Butch."

"Dude is his name, and he likes it." Jason stands, dusts off his hand, and then pushes his bike through the gates. He whistles and jerks his head as a sign to follow him, and I assume he means the dog until his eyes flick to me and he mutters, "Don't just stand there scratchin' your peach, move it."

Dude groans and turns to follow his master. *Is this what it's come to? I'm Jason's property, and he's now my master.* As much as I dislike being whistled at like a dog, I follow Jason down the winding dirt track, which leads to the riverside, just like Jason said. And lo and behold, there's an abandoned factory that nature is trying to claw back with a vengeance. Leafy vines coil around the iron railings and poke through some of the broken windows like nature is swallowing it whole. Either the glass has been tinted, or someone spray painted it black. It looks kind of foreboding. I cast a critical eye over it, thinking it could be the perfect setting for a horror movie. Jason pushes his bike inside, and the dog bounds in after him, leaving me out here with nothing but the sound of the wind rustling through the tall grass. I hear female laughter from inside the dilapidated factory, which reassures me. Bodie said the guys all have girlfriends. I'm a little nervous about running into Ivy, the girl he used to gush about. Bodie was crazy about her and even asked our mom if he could have our grandmother's old engagement ring because he planned to propose. My chest tightens as I revisit the memory.

Jason points to a woman's bra dangling from the handlebars of Tex's bike. "That's nothing," he attempts to reassure me. "You'll probably see all kinds of things you'll wish you could unsee, but it's all part of club life as you're about to find out."

From the frantic sex noises coming from some-where inside, I'd say someone was having a quickie. I try not to look so embarrassed as I walk through the hall and into the communal living space, seeing Tex's jeans around his ankles, and his bare ass banging against his girlfriend as she clings to him like a monkey. Everyone else is ignoring it, so I do too. There's no way I could ever do anything remotely like that in front of other people. I'm not a prude. I'm just private. Not like I'll get much privacy in this open-plan space. It's industrial and echoey. There's a metal staircase leading to an upper level that overlooks the communal area, and on the ground floor, right at the back, I notice they've done a good job at installing a kitchen. It's made up of stainless-steel worktops, cupboards with sliding doors, a commercial-sized fridge, and one of those chef's stoves you'd find in a restaurant. I grimace with disgust as Rooster lights his cigarette on the hob, then flicks ash in the sink. That's just gross. I might be a grease monkey, but at least I'm housetrained.

"I thought you said this place was decent?" I comment, scrutinizing their living standards.

Jason drags his fingers through his hair, looking slightly embarrassed. I can tell by the shocked look in his eyes that he didn't expect to walk into a bombsite.

"Sorry about this, Peaches," Jason mutters, thrown

off his stride for a moment. He drags his tongue over his bottom lip, then whistles loud enough to rattle our ears. "Hey! Is this a fucking pigsty or a clubhouse? Clean up your shit by the time I come back downstairs or else you'll be sleeping outside under the stars. Don't think I'm kidding. There's already one ass on my hitlist." He takes my hand and leads me upstairs.

I look down from the railings and see three women scurrying around, throwing all their takeout cartons in the trash. The guys are helping, but there's a fourth woman, a long-haired brunette who catches my eye. She doesn't get up from the ratty sofa. Our eyes meet briefly as she looks at me, her hand resting reflexively on her prominent baby bump. My words get snagged in my throat, recognizing her from the photo on Bodie's workstation. That's Ivy. His girlfriend – his pregnant girlfriend. Oh my god.

Jason unlocks the first door we reach. "In here," he says, his tone gruff. "Before we do anything else, we should talk."

CHAPTER FIVE

Jason brings me inside what I assume is his bedroom, turns on a lamp, then opens the window to let some fresh air in. It's too late for him to hide the fact that he smokes weed. He kicks the makeshift ashtray beneath the armchair in the corner of the room to conceal it from view, but it's pointless because I hear the rusty tin can scrape across the wood. I'll be the first to admit I'm not the tidiest person in the world. My disorganized workstation is proof of that. But when I get up in the morning, I bother to make the damn bed.

"I didn't know you were such a slob," I remark, looking around at all the laundry dumped in the corner, with T-shirts and jeans incongruously strewn all over the chair. "How can you tell which is clean or dirty? Do you just sniff it?"

Jason grins sheepishly as I call him out. "I wasn't expecting company. You've just caught me on a bad day."

"Is that so?" I drag my eyes around the room. "Your mom will throw a bitch fit if she sees where you're living."

It's true. Liv Knight runs the beauty salon in town. She's immaculate, which is probably why Sheriff Dan can't help himself. He keeps sniffing around like a dog, marking his territory around the middle-aged spinster. Jason's family home is only a few streets away from where I live. He moved from the dumpy side of town after his mom scraped enough cash together to save for a downpayment on a house. Liv has never been married; hence the reason Jason carries her maiden name. No one knows who his father is. Liv would never say. But one thing's for sure, he doesn't look anything like Sheriff Dan. It's funny, when I mention his mom, it makes Jason's eyebrows almost fly off his face.

"Hey, leave her out of this," Jason mutters, then dumps the pile of clothes back onto the chair. "Unless you want me to call your parents to tell them about the stunt you pulled tonight." He eyes me doubtfully.

I roll my eyes, then puff out a breath. "Well, if you think I'm spending my time cleaning up after you, you've got another thing coming."

"I don't expect you to, Peaches." Jason steps on the back of his heel to remove his boot, then perches on the armchair to pull off the other one. They both land on the floor with a thump. "Just pick up after yourself. We don't invade each other's personal space unless we're invited. But as for the clubhouse." He nods his head at the door, hinting at the communal space downstairs. "It's a team effort to keep it clean. Nobody rides for free. We all contribute toward the beers and smokes. The girls shop for groceries and take care of the laundry. Not just because they're women, but because they say we're no good at that shit. I'll introduce you properly in a bit. They'll all be dying to meet you."

"Ah, so that's why your laundry pile resembles Mount Everest, because no one can come into your room without permission." I quirk my lips as I look around. "You know, maybe you should practice what you preach." I shrug. "Lead by example instead of just barking orders at people. If they see you living like a bum, they'll follow suit."

Jason goes to speak but clamps his mouth shut,

unable to disagree. He rubs his elbow, his expression darkening.

"I haven't been in a good place since, you know." He breaks eye contact, dropping his gaze. "You of all people should know."

"Yeah, I miss Bodie so much it physically hurts me to think about him." I stare straight at Jason, noticing the way his eyes keep darting my way. "But the way I see it is I could spend my whole life wallowing in my room, barely existing, or I can get off my ass and find the fucker who shot him."

Jason drives his hands through his hair and turns away from me. "I told you; I'm handling it."

The signs of depression and grief are all around us. It looks like Jason hit rock bottom a long time ago. The top of his dresser is full of cologne bottles, a collection of deodorant tubes, empty cigarette packets, receipts Jason had scrunched and left there to gather dust, and a collection of beer bottles that have dead flies and cigarette butts floating around inside the remnants. I turn around and kick something by accident; it's a beard trimmer Jason left on the floor, plugged into the charger. There's a lot of crap lying around on the floor. It's hard to tell what's trash and what's worth keeping. If this fucker thinks I'm moving in with him, he's in for a rude awakening. He may rule the roost out there with his biker buddies, but behind closed doors, we should lay down some rules to respect each other's boundaries. Just because I'm hopelessly besotted with the handsome slob, whose hypocrisy makes me want to throw him off the balcony and grab a broom and a duster, I'm nobody's bitch. I have a full-time job to go back to. I'm the boss. If the Hawks want to continue to work there, they'll be working for me. Not Jason.

"If this is how it's going to be, then this isn't going to work." I sit on the edge of his crumpled bed.

Jason scowls over his shoulder. "I've warned you about that mouth of yours. Unless you've got something nice to say, I can think of a great way to plug it."

"I'd love to see you try," I answer back without thinking. The words just fly out of my mouth before I can catch them.

Jason's hands drop to his front, the sharp sound of his zipper tearing through my ears as I realize he's taking off his pants. To do what? To follow through with his threat?

"Wait, I'm sorry," I rush to say as he shoves his jeans down his legs, then steps out of them.

"Too late, Peaches," Jason rasps, pulling his vest over his head and tossing it onto the laundry pile.

My breath catches as he turns around and I get a

good look at his godly, inked body, my eyes bulging at his pierced appendage. The guy oozes power and authority without even having a stitch on. How is that possible? He's intimidating to look at.

"Now's not the time to be shy," Jason says, stepping closer and moving a small stack of bike magazines with his bare foot. "When you dare someone to do something, you've got to see it through. If you don't, your opinion doesn't count for shit. I warned you before we started this that there'd be repercussions for giving me lip. I won't stand for any backchat. Either you haven't been listening, or you're a glutton for punishment."

I hold up my hand in front of me. "Just let me speak, please."

Jason stops right in front of me and crouches down, resting on one knee. His blank expression is unreadable. I hate that I can't tell what he's thinking. I wish I could read his mind and find out if he's telling the truth. That he's always liked me. If there's even the smallest chance that anything he's said to me is true, I will snatch that and run with it. It's the first time in a long time I haven't felt so alone.

"Just tell me because I need to know." I reach out and hold his face between my hands, looking him right in the eyes. "I need you to be honest with me. No secrets. No lies. Is everything you've said tonight true? Do you have real feelings for me?"

Without hesitation, Jason replies, "Yes." My eyes twitch at the corners. "I love you, Keira," he clarifies, erasing my doubts.

It takes me a moment to process the weight of that revelation and work out what this means for us. It means more to me than I initially thought. My heart thumps a little harder, swelling with relief.

"I love you too," I reply, blinking back my emotions. "Then I can trust you'll do what's right by Bodie and help me to nail that son of a bitch."

Jason scrunches his eyes shut and huffs with agitation. "Not this again." In a swift action, he's on the bed, pulling me across his lap, face down so that my forehead is almost touching the floor.

"Jason!" I wail, not expecting him to yank me over his lap like that.

"You're gonna listen to me, so help me God." Jason rubs his hand against my bruised denim-clad bottom.

I flip like a fish as he wrestles my jeans and panties over my hips and bares my ass. He doesn't stop there. This time, he shoves two fingers inside my pussy, making my eyes bulge as his thumb presses firmly against my asshole. The bastard is holding me like a bowling ball, his thumb applying pressure to my ring of fire until it bursts through my resistance.

"Argh! What the fuck?!" I screech, tears pricking my eyes.

Jason moves his fingers until the pressure stops and the pleasure begins. "You're mine, Keira. Mine to love and protect. It's my job to stop you from doing shit that'll get you hurt or worse . . . killed. I don't want you going anywhere near that psychopath. Do you hear me?"

I'm too busy moaning as he fingers me. He removes his fingers and smacks me hard on the ass, the sharp sting and loud slap making me jolt across his lap.

"Answer me," Jason commands, sounding angry.

"But—" I don't get the chance to finish before he smacks me again, only this time much harder.

"Ow," I cry out.

"The Jackals won't think twice about putting you down. Don't you get it? If something happens to you, I'll be better off dead," Jason lectures me, his voice cracking with emotion at the end. "I can't lose you. I just can't." He rubs away the fire on my skin, caressing away the stinging sensation until the heat on my ass and the warmth of his palm become one. "You've just got to trust me to do what needs to be done. Please,

Peaches. If you just stay out of it, everything will work out fine. I promise you. It'll all work out fine."

Tears cling to the tip of my nose, tickling the end of it, making it itch. I wipe my hand over my face as Jason allows me to stand.

"Fine, I'll drop it," I concede with a sob, moving to pull up my pants.

Jason's hand darts out to stop me, then leans forward to press his lips against my stomach. Instinctively, my hands rest upon his head, fingers driving into his hair as he descends to my mound while peppering me with soft kisses.

"Thank you," Jason aspirates with a warm, tickling breath.

This tender moment is enough to plug the gap in my heart for now, which is strange for me since I'm not usually the type of girl who needs hugs and reassurance. Just that one time when my world came crashing down. Jason was there to catch me when I fell, holding me until I could sleep. Maybe at first he saw me as his best friend's little sister, but somewhere along the way, I wormed my way inside his heart. It's like we are meant to be. No other man has this effect on me. When Jason holds me, I don't jerk away. I melt into his embrace and draw strength from him. There's only

Jason who can comfort me and make me feel whole and safe.

"Is it good when I touch you here? Or maybe here?" Jason murmurs as he kisses me, his warm breath billowing against my skin.

My legs tremble as he parts my folds with his thumbs and drags the tip of his tongue across my clit.

"Right there," I answer, fisting his hair.

"Keep watching," he commands, flicking out his tongue for another lick.

Jason doesn't check that I'm looking as he feasts, too busy tasting me, his fluttering tongue driving me to the brink of insanity. But he expects me to watch, and if I disobey, he might stop, and if he stops, I'll die. I need this. It's my ultimate fantasy. I've been needing this for so long.

"Uh," I gasp, fighting the urge to close my eyes and drown in an ocean of bliss.

The tension inside me builds, skittering through my nerves until it bursts right out. He whirls me around. My eyes scrunch shut as my back hits the mattress, and Jason climbs over me, covering me with his magnificent heft, notches his pierced cock at my pussy, then shoves deep inside. The bed creaks as he thrusts, slow at first, but then he quickens his pace, his ass bouncing, strong arms caging me in, his mouth open, his face pinched with pure pleasure.

"God, you feel amazing," Jason groans, curling one hand around my throat, his grip tightening. "If it becomes too much, just tap out."

"Don't hold back," I say. "Fuck me hard." It's what I need, and he knows it.

With my full permission, Jason gives me what I want. The headboard knocks against the wall the harder he thrusts, and my breath thins from the constriction around my throat. I feel everything. The immense stretch of his big, thick cock, and the stainless-steel embellishments rubbing against my G-spot. Holy hell, the guy knows how to fuck. My imagination could never do him justice. Lights burst in my eyes; the rest of my body switches off and sends heightened sensations straight to my pussy. I can't breathe, but the intense fucking feels amazing. Just when I think I'm going to black out, Jason releases his grip and air rushes straight into my lungs, the most incredible climax hits me, and all I can see is stars.

"Fuck," Jason barks his release, hips jerking as he cums.

The intense rush leaves me stuck between hyperventilating and sobbing. My head is spinning so fast the room zooms in and out of focus.

"I know, baby, I know. I'm right here. Just breathe." Jason holds me, rolling me onto his chest.

Exhaustion washes over me, and I close my eyes. I only intend to rest for a few minutes. But when I open them again, pale sunlight pools in through the gap in the curtains, meaning I must have slept through the night. I glance up, peeling my cheek from Jason's muscular chest, and find him sound asleep, his dark crescent lashes fanned out against his skin. Smiling fondly, I trace the strong, angular profile of his nose, the excitement fluttering in the pit of my stomach about having a future with this man.

CHAPTER SIX

"Are you gonna get up and let me take a piss, or are you just gonna keep staring like a creep?" Jason mumbles in a sleep-roughened voice.

I lean up to give him a good morning kiss, which he reciprocates lovingly. "You're cute when you're sleeping," I comment.

Jason rolls his eyes. "You're cute when you shut your mouth," he retorts. "Wanna share a shower?" he offers, changing the subject.

A shower sounds great after working up a sweat last night. We take an unhurried shower, spending way too long beneath the faucet getting dirty and clean at the same time. I'm exhausted by the time he's finished pounding into me. My back is chafed raw from being rubbed against the cold tiles. Before the hot water runs out, we get out. We dry off, and I put on yesterday's clothes, not feeling too good about wearing the same underwear. After I rake out the snags in my hair with my fingers, I rummage through my purse for some mascara. My puffy eyes are proof of a good night's sleep, and now I feel rested and refreshed, better than I've felt in a long time. I catch Jason sniffing a dark gray T-shirt before putting it on. He sees me smirking and shakes his head sheepishly.

"You're such a slob," I say, chuckling.

"Yeah, yeah." He grins. "Are you ready to meet the crew?" Jason asks, while doing up the fly of his jeans.

I already know the guys. It's their girlfriends I'm unfamiliar with. And if I'm being honest, I'm nervous about meeting Ivy.

"Sure, I could use some breakfast after our vigorous workout," I reply, rubbing my abdomen gingerly.

Jason winces, and I guess that means we all fend for ourselves. "The fridge is full of beer and not much else. But if you're lucky there might be some leftover pizza in the box."

"Forget it," I answer, waving my hand in dismissal. "I'll grab something from home."

I notice him bristling as I mention home, but don't think too much about it. My tongue is drier than the Sahara Desert, and I'm in desperate need of some coffee. If he doesn't have that, then I'll kick his ass. Jason brings me downstairs and puts on the radio, cranking up the volume as a hint for everyone to wake the fuck up. At least everywhere is cleaner than it was last night. I can tell Jason tried to make this rundown factory a home away from home, with shabby mismatched couches that have seen the best of their days, a grubby pool table with ominous stains on the red felt, a makeshift bar built from old pallet wood, and a flat-screen TV in the middle of the room with a trailing extension wire that disappears behind a stack of boxes against the wall. It's not the Ritz by any means, but it's a base to lay low for a while. The loud rock music alerts the dog to our presence; he barks from one of the upstairs rooms. Someone lets him out, and he bounds down the industrial staircase to greet us.

"Let him out before he craps everywhere," Rooster hollers over the balcony railing, letting me know his room is the one next to Jason's.

One by one, the guys emerge from their rooms with their bed-ragged girlfriends behind them. The only one I don't see is Ivy who has the perfect excuse to stay in bed.

"Everybody, listen up!" Jason hollers. "We've got a

new houseguest. I know some of you already know Ratchet's kid sister, Kiera. But those of you who don't, I'd like you to come down and meet her. And before you get any crazy ideas about inviting her to join you for sex. Don't. She's off-limits."

I can't tell if the last part was meant as a joke or not.

My eyes cut to Jason. "I'll stay over occasionally, but I'm not moving in. No way." I don't mean to sound rude, but I prefer my home comforts.

An unladylike cackle shatters the silence upstairs. "She's got the right idea. This place is a dump," one of the women says.

When I eventually look up, I see three women all grinning down at us. Tex comes downstairs wearing his boxer shorts. He pulls a brunette onto his lap as he sits on the couch. I think she's wearing one of his massive T-shirts as a nightdress and presumably nothing else because she's paranoid about flashing me her ass. Rooster leans against the pool table in nothing but a pair of light gray sweatpants and socks. He's cuddling a petite redhead who's wearing a hot rock-burned bedsheet like a toga. Hustle and a pretty blonde are the only ones respectfully dressed. His woman has almost as many tattoos as Jason does. Dude bounds over to where Tex is sitting and plonks his ass down by his bare feet, Dude's head nudging Tex's leg as a hint for Tex to pet him.

Tex pets the dog, then his eyes cut to me. "Don't be such a stubborn little bitch. It won't be safe for you to live at your folks' place alone. Especially now." He rolls his eyes sarcastically. "You're safer here with us."

I look at Jason. "What does he mean, *safer*?"

"Thank you, Tex," Jason drawls in a warning tone, then looks at me, and I notice the flinch in his eyes. "We haven't exactly ironed out all the details as such. I'll get to that in a minute."

Well, that sounds ominous. Why would I be in danger? I haven't done anything wrong. Surely, I would be in deeper shit if I stayed here with the culprits of last night's bar fight. I need to get back to work. I don't want these guys bringing trouble to my doorstep. If that's the case, I'll run Dad's garage single-handed.

"Keira." Jason turns to me, snaking his arm around my waist. "There's nothing for you to be worried about. We're all family here. You already know Tex." The hulking mountain of muscle grunts obnoxiously. He's the only member of the Hawks to keep his actual name.

Jason continues with the introduction, "The sour-faced bitch on his lap is Carly, also known as Claws. Don't piss her off or she'll scratch your eyes out. And then there's Hustle." I know his real name is Huey, but he absolutely fucking hates it. The silver-tongued heartthrob has the gift of the gab and could charm the panties off a man-hating battle-ax, he's so good-looking. "And his woman, Tess, who we call Tequila because she can drink like a fish and still swim in a straight line," Jason introduces the pretty inked blonde who returns a friendly smile. "Last but not least, Rooster's old lady, Stevie, who we all know earned the name Soapbox because of her righteous preaching." Jason gestures to Ryan's woman. The guys have always called Ryan by his last name, Rooster.

Stevie raises her eyebrows at Jason. "Excuse me, but I can't help it if I'm always right."

Jason exhales nasally. "Since you're so fond of preaching, you can tell Kiera the rules."

Stevie doesn't hesitate to take center stage, sitting up straight with an air of superiority. "The rules around here are simple. Don't take what doesn't belong to you. Partners included. Ask first. Don't be a dick. Respect one another, and they'll respect you. We're a family. We watch each other's backs. If we have a problem, we take it to Havoc. We don't discuss club business outside of the clubhouse. If we fuck up, we get punished. End of story." She shrugs.

"You forgot one. Ask no questions and they'll tell you no lies?" a woman speaks from the balcony in a cynical tone.

I glance up and see Ivy leaning on the railings. Who knows how long she's been standing there listening, the stains of grief visible for all to see in her sunken eyes. She glares at Jason as if she was talking about him. But Jason doesn't rise to it. If anything, he dismisses it completely.

"Stiletto, Bodie's old lady," Jason introduces the dark-haired, sad-eyed beauty. It feels awkward to be meeting her for the first time under these circumstances. She didn't show at Bodie's funeral, so I assumed they weren't as serious as Bodie made out. She's carrying around so much anger, and I can't say I blame her. When was he planning to spring this on us? After she gave birth? Our parents are going to freak out when I tell them. They would want to be here to support her through it all. I certainly will, whether she wants me to or not. I'll win the aunt of the year award; I'll love that kid so hard.

"Hi, you must be Ivy. It's so nice to finally meet you," I blurt out, trying to alleviate the tension.

"Yeah, nice," Ivy huffs, her tone bitter and hostile. "We should raise a toast to celebrate." She rolls her eyes, then goes back to her room and slams the door hard enough to make me flinch.

"Oh my god, I didn't mean to upset her," I utter, turning to Jason. "Maybe I should go after her and apologize?"

Jason shakes his head, his eyes creasing at the corners. "Nah, leave her be. It isn't you she's mad at. It's me."

Hm. I wonder why?

Tex snorts. "We're all cut up about Bodie. But if Stiletto is gonna be pissed at anyone, it should be Mayor Booker and that fuckwit, Marcus Jackal."

"Mayor Booker?" I blurt out, noticing Jason bristling beside me.

Is Tex insinuating it was the mayor who gave Marcus an alibi because they're in cahoots?

"The mayor can't see straight without his glasses," Jason cuts in dismissively. "All that matters is that Marcus gets what's coming to him." He dips his gaze at me. "Do you wanna go somewhere for breakfast?"

I look down at yesterday's clothes and grimace. "Nah, just take me home, thanks."

Jason nods.

"Do you want some coffee first?" Stevie asks.

"Sure," I reply, following her to the kitchenette.

Something tells me Stevie likes to gossip, and that's

fine by me. She can run her mouth all she likes. To hell with the club code. It sounds like they fray the edges of the truth, only sharing information on a need-to-know basis. Jason can't be around me all the time. He isn't my personal bodyguard.

"It won't take too long to brew," Stevie mentions as she works. "Don't mind the noise. It works just fine."

A few seconds after she switches on the machine, it starts clunking like the nuts and bolts are churning around in the coffee grinder. I put my hands over my ears until it quiets down and starts hissing.

"I'm putting in a complaint to the Prez," I joke. "He ought to dig deep and buy the club a new one."

Stevie chuckles. "Oh, man, if only he pulled that Robin Hood shit for the benefit of the club and not the community, we'd be rolling in dough."

My eyes twitch, and I glance over my shoulder to check Jason isn't listening. He's busy reprimanding Tex for running his mouth at me, which means I'm free to poke Stevie for information.

"Look, Stevie, can you help me out with something?" I say, cringing. "I wasn't listening to what Havoc said to me while he was giving me an ass whooping. Something about the mayor and the Jackals. I really don't think I can take another spanking today. Can you fill in the gaps?"

Stevie's lips twist into a wry smile. "Fine, I'll help you out. You can owe me one when I need a favor."

"Thank you." I sigh with relief.

Stevie leans closer. "Well, think of Marcus Jackal as the Sheriff of Nottingham, and Mayor Booker as Prince John." She continues to rhyme off characters, assigning names to members of the Hawks like she's telling the most compelling story of the century. "Mayor Booker approached Havoc first, wanting to recruit some hired muscle to force the residents of Mountview to sell their land to developers. When Havoc told him to go fuck himself, the Jackals rode into town. The Hawks have been doing everything they can to stop them, but it's our word against the mayor's."

Maintaining a stoic expression, not wanting her to see how shocked I am, I spare a quick glance at Jason, resenting him for not trusting me with that vital piece of information. If the Mayor wants our land, then my garage is on the hit list. What am I doing wasting time waiting around for coffee? I need to tell Sheriff Dan.

"I think I'll pass on the coffee," I say to Stevie. "Thanks anyway."

Her face sags with disappointment. "Oh, okay."

Jason takes me home, and we share an awkward goodbye kiss on my doorstep. I fake being fine just to get him to drive away and leave me be, but the minute he turns his back, my smile melts off my face faster than ice cream on a hot day. *That conniving son of a bitch.* I don't know what it is with men like him thinking they can protect us women from the truth. I'm not a delicate flower. I'm like a thorn. And believe me, no one wants one of those stuck in their side.

CHAPTER SEVEN

After some much-needed coffee and a cream cheese bagel, I take another shower and change into something comfortable. It's not like I'm out to impress anyone in my lounge pants and hoodie. I have things to do, people to see, and a vendetta to plan for the mayor. If the people of Mountview knew what he was doing, they'd run him out of town. But it'll be hard to get people to listen. Politicians are known for telling lies, but people voted for Booker because he grew up here. They trust him and are disillusioned into thinking he wants the best for them and this town when all he really wants is to line his own greedy pockets. But for some reason, Sheriff Dan keeps calling him out on his bullshit, so I'm hoping there's still one guy left in Mountview with a shred of integrity. I dial his number and wait for him or either one of his deputies to pick up the call.

"Hello, Sheriff Lopez speaking," Dan answers, but he sounds breathless like he's just stopped running.

"Oh, is it a bad time?" I ask, hoping I haven't unwittingly aided and abetted a criminal's escape or worse, disturbed him during happy time with Liv. "I'm sorry to disturb you, sir. It's Keira Blake. You said to call you if I ever needed anything."

Nah, there's no way Dan would answer the phone if he was that busy. He was probably working out.

"It's fine, Keira. What's the problem?" he answers exhaustedly.

I start awkwardly pacing around the kitchen, thinking about how best to explain this. "I have some information about Mayor Booker and Marcus Jackal," I say, hearing Dan's weary sigh rattling down the line. "What if Booker helped Marcus with an alibi the night of my brother's murder because Marcus is working for him? Uh . . . I heard through a friend that Booker is paying the Jackals to scare people into leaving town. They seem to think he's got something going on with the developers who want to buy the land around here."

"They're not developers," Dan says flatly. "They are oil miners. Hence the reason the Jackals are being so pushy. Booker is set to make a fortune from this."

"If you knew what Booker was up to, why haven't you done anything about it?" I ask critically.

"Look, Keira," Dan says with a resigned sigh. "I'm gonna need you to drop it and let me handle Booker."

"I don't know who's worse. You or Jason," I retort with an annoyed huff. "All I'm getting is a wall of secrecy. Your influence has rubbed off on him."

"You ought to listen to him. Don't go poking your nose around in Booker's business. You'll only get hurt," Dan warns me.

"Like my brother, you mean?" I snap back.

Dan's exasperated exhale rattles down the line like crackling static. "I'm not asking you. I'm telling you to stay out of it and let us handle it. Just go about your business and keep your head down. Jason knows what he's doing. You should listen to him."

"Well, thanks for nothing, asshole." I hang up the phone and slump against the kitchen counter, weighing up my options.

It seems like Sheriff Dan and Jason have made plans. I just wish they'd share them with me. Those Jackal bastards have caused Mountview enough misery. They took my brother from me, from Ivy and their child, and from Mom and Dad too. I want retribution. An eye for an eye. A tooth for a tooth. I want to see

Marcus Jackal take his last breath, then I can spit on his grave. Maybe then I'll find peace.

My phone rings. It's Jason. I roll my eyes, inwardly cursing at Sheriff Dan for calling him. There's no way it can be a coincidence. When I don't answer the first time, he calls again, and again. When I don't answer those calls, that's when the texts and voicemails start rolling in. I'm not interested in being told what to do. My mind is spinning, absorbing all the information I brushed off as nothing. The time those Jackal assholes came into the garage and threatened Bodie should still be on the CCTV recording unless someone has deleted it. So, that's the first place I go.

The roads are quiet. I don't see anyone loitering around as I let myself in and gather the pile of mail from off the floor. Just a handful of bills. Nothing else. I go into the office and skim through the files. Everything is on the computer, all saved on the cloud account. There's no reason for anyone to have tampered with it. I'm pleased to find the file I'm looking for, but all I can make out from the audio is just muffled voices and the occasional word. Why do guys mumble when they talk? Their hands covering their mouths when they scratch their stubble makes it harder to lip-read what they're saying.

A metallic thump like the sound of a gas canister

falling onto concrete alerts me to the workshop. There's no way anything could have fallen on its own. It had to have been pushed.

"Hello?" I call through the open doorway, getting up from the desk chair. "Is there somebody there?"

I hear the rustling of clothing like someone is walking quickly, and I dart to the window to see who it is. Movement catches my eye behind the hydraulic ramp as if someone just crouched down behind a small stack of tires. I send a quick text to Jason, telling him where I am and hoping that he's on his way over to find me.

"We're closed," I feebly shout, my eyes following a long, wet trail on the floor and seeing the top of the crouched person's head moving toward the exit behind all the shelving racks.

Gasoline fumes reach my nostrils, sending my senses on high alert. Another splash of clear liquid hits the floor as whoever it is leaves. I can tell it's a guy from his build. His face is covered with a bandanna, and he's not alone. His accomplice is wearing a similar face covering, and he tosses the plastic canister into the garage, then flicks open a lighter, his gloved finger resting on top of the flint wheel.

"Please, don't do it!" I beg.

With all the flammable liquids stocked here, the garage will go up like a rocket.

"You can thank your boyfriend, Havoc," the masked moron replies. "The boss wants to send him a message."

"Well then text him like a normal person," I plead, hoping I can keep him talking long enough for me to hit the fire alarm button and set off the sprinkler system. I'm not bothered about fucking up the machinery because I'm insured to the hilt. Unfortunately, my life doesn't have a reset switch.

I'm about to break the glass with my elbow as he tosses the lighter onto the floor, igniting a whoosh of yellow flames. There should be water pouring from the ceiling, but the sprinklers aren't working. Someone has disabled it. The smoke and heat swallow the air within seconds.

"Help!" I shout, diving onto the carpet as the front door slams shut. There's no way out from inside the office. The back exit is on the opposite side of the workshop. I call Jason, but the call goes straight through to voicemail. He read my text, so he must be on his way. Stretching the neckline of my hoodie, I use it to cover my airways and crawl beneath the choking smoke to escape. I can't see past the end of my nose, eyes streaming, throat closing, and my lungs ablaze.

Breathing is impossible. But then the rear door flies open, siphoning half the smoke. I don't see my savior until we're outside in the yard after they drag me out. The leather-clad biker is wearing a helmet with the visor down, so I don't know who it is, but they're wearing the same outfit as the mysterious stalker who's been keeping tabs on me since Bodie died. My eyes roll into the back of my skull, and I hear sirens wailing somewhere in the distance. I must have passed out cold for a while because when I open my eyes again, I'm in the hospital. My throat hurts, and every breath I take feels like my lungs are filtering shards of glass.

"Keira, thank God." Jason's voice makes my eyes dart to the left of me, and I see him sitting beside me, slumped over my bed, and holding my hand. "What the fuck were you thinking, going to the garage alone? Dan called, and he said you sounded upset. I thought we resolved this. We went over it this morning, and you said you trusted me enough to handle things."

It takes me a while to answer, grimacing with tears. But when I eventually start to speak, my voice is strained and hoarse. "How was I supposed to know that Dan knew? I just wanted to help. So, I went to the garage to check the footage from the day those guys showed up and threatened you and Bodie. I thought they might have said something that Dan could use in court. The next thing I know, the garage is on fire, and I'm in the hospital."

Jason kisses my hand, presses it to his cheek, then looks at me, his brows dimpled with worry. "You could have been killed."

"I know." The reality of it churns my stomach with nausea. "But thankfully, someone saw what was happening, and they were quick to pull me out."

"Who?" Jason asks, bristling with suspicion.

"I don't know. I couldn't see who it was. But I recognize the biker leathers and helmet as the same person who keeps cruising past the garage."

Jason's eyes twitch questioningly, not liking the idea of someone watching me. "You were alone when I got there seconds before the cops showed up."

"I didn't drag myself out. I know what I saw," I reply bluntly.

Jason blinks. "I know you did, baby. It doesn't matter. All that matters is that you're safe." He reaches across the bed to stroke my hair, then hovers over me to kiss my forehead. "I'm just gonna step outside for a minute to check on something. I'll be right back."

CHAPTER EIGHT

I'm bored out of my wits. The doctor insisted on keeping me in for a week, but the way Jason refuses to leave my side, anyone would think I only have days left to live. He's been getting on the nurses' last nerves, refusing to leave the room during examinations, bombarding the doctor with annoying questions, and even insisting on bringing in food for me in case someone at the hospital kitchen tries to poison me. Jason's paranoia has been on high alert since the attack. It's embarrassing, but I know he means well. When I look into his eyes, I see the devil staring back. Lethal and besotted. Crazy in love. I know he'd kill for me. He'd go to the depths of hell to keep me safe. It's what I always wanted. A big, strong man who will sweep me into his arms and love me forever. No other guy has ever come close.

Someone knocks, and Jason stalks to the door to answer it. I hear mumbling male voices, then someone hands him a bag.

"Hey, Peaches. I asked the guys to call by your house to pick up some things for you." My eyes bulge at the thought of them snooping around all my private belongings. *I have secret things inside my dresser drawers that I don't want anybody else to see.* Least of all Tex. I can imagine him holding my vibrator and clicking through all the settings. The thought makes me cringe and wish the bed would swallow me whole. "Don't worry, they didn't rummage through your underwear drawer. Soapbox did that. She picked out something comfortable for you to wear when the doc is ready to discharge you," Jason reassures me, setting the bag down beside the bed.

I flash a grateful smile, relieved to hear it. "I appreciate that."

Jason seems fidgety today. It's like he can't keep still. He checks my phone to see if it's finished charging, and I can tell it has because he removes the cable. Aside from a cracked screen, my phone still works, which I'm glad about. Like the garage, it's insured. I'll get a new handset and transfer all my apps and photos.

I have so many treasured memories stored on the device that it will break my heart if I lose them.

"Do you want to text your mom?" Jason asks, holding out my phone.

I reach out to take it, then text Mom, telling her that everything is fine. I don't call in case the doctor or one of the nurses walks in. Mom will overhear and wonder what's going on. She doesn't need to know about the arson attack, or that I'm at the hospital. She'd only worry, and so would Dad. Lying to her makes me sick to my stomach, but the last thing I want is for her and Dad to rush home. They are better off staying away, far away where Mayor Booker and his Jackal henchmen can't get their filthy hands on them. My phone beeps with an incoming text that I read, then resume a relaxed position.

"My mom and dad say hi. I told them you and the guys have been helping me at the garage." I swallow thickly. At least it isn't a total lie. "She's glad I have you guys, but I'm scared Dad will want to come back to check how I'm doing. I'll need to file an insurance claim when I get home."

"You don't need to worry about that right now. The Hawks will help," Jason says reassuringly. "You're one of us. We take care of each other."

"I appreciate that; thank you," I reply, opening my arms as he leans down to hug me.

Jason's cologne fills my airways, and it calms me. Not only do the Hawks look out for one another, but the mysterious biker who pulled me out of the fire must be a guardian angel that was sent down from heaven to watch over me. His identity remains to be seen. I wish he could have stuck around long enough for Jason to arrive, but maybe he didn't want to be questioned by cops. Maybe he was worried Sheriff Dan would think he had something to do with it. For all I know, there's another vigilante out there protecting the good people of Mountview.

A phone rings. It isn't mine. Jason pulls away and looks at the screen, his brows pinched as he frowns. He hasn't swiped to reject the call like he usually does whenever he can't be bothered to answer. It's one of those rare occasions when he steps outside to answer it, and that pisses me off. I try not to show it as he comes back, shoving his phone inside his jacket pocket like everything's fine.

"I got some good news and some bad news, Peaches," Jason says, not meeting my gaze. "The bad news is that you're not going home until tomorrow. Doctor's orders. And the good news is I'm gonna confront that fucker, Marcus Jackal, tonight."

My heart jolts with shock, and I sit up in bed. "Oh, and that's not a coincidence?" I glare at Jason. "You're going after Marcus, and you've told the doctor to keep me in one more night."

This triggers Jason's annoyance, and his eyes flash into a pointed stare. "Damn right you're staying here where it's safe," he's quick to answer, jabbing his finger at the floor. "Don't you dare even think about discharging yourself, or so help me, you won't sit for a month by the time I'm through with you."

It takes me an awful amount of restraint not to react to his alpha male rant because I know it will only escalate matters, and this is not the time nor the place to argue. I'm aware of the other patients in the ward outside this room, and I'm sure they don't want to hear me being spanked or castigated by an overprotective biker. It's unfair to disturb their peace when I know this is an argument I'll never win. So, I sit here and keep my mouth shut, plotting silently and secretly around his rules just to appease his stupid male ego. There's no point fueling his fire with more anger. And probing him for questions will only rile him up. So, I do neither. Instead, I pull on his heartstrings, putting my best acting abilities to good use, pretending to be wounded by his comment, taking my mind to a sad place where people are cruel to little puppies so the tears in my eyes seem genuine. And it works. The first ragged intake of breath is enough to make Jason stop mid-rant to console me. It's nice when he cuddles and reassures me. I would rather him pepper me with sweet kisses than scowl at me with contempt. I blink once, and hot tears roll down my cheeks. Someone better hand me an Oscar. I'm playing Jason Knight like a fiddle, and he doesn't even know it.

"Aw, come on. Don't do that, Peaches," Jason says, fussing around me. "I'm sorry I yelled."

I wipe my eyes with my hands. "I think you should go."

"Peaches." Jason tries to cuddle me tighter, but I refuse to let him hold me.

He lets go, visibly upset by this.

"I don't think I can do this," I say, my voice straining with emotion.

Jason blanches, his expression freezing with dread. "What are you talking about? You're my girl. I fuckin' love you."

He forces his way onto the bed, and I have no choice other than to move over to accommodate him. It's either that or he'll scoop me up and haul me onto his lap, and I'm not wearing panties beneath my nightdress.

"You keep secrets from me, and I'm just supposed

to accept it," I complain, letting him snuggle against me, wrapping his arms around me, which I allow him do this time. "But if I kept things from you, you'd go all caveman on my ass."

Jason involuntarily chuckles at my comment. He must know it's inappropriate to laugh by the way he quickly recovers from it. I'm supposed to be mad at him, and he wants to redeem himself. "Baby, your ass is off limits until you're fully healed. I said I'd take care of you, so please don't fight me on this."

I can feel Jason's heart thumping wildly in his chest against my cheek. Is he afraid of losing me, or is there something else rattling him?

"I've got a gut feeling there's something else you're not telling me," I mention, feeling his posture stiffen. "Just tell me what it is. I promise I won't do anything stupid, but I need to know. Are you planning to kill Marcus? Is that what you mean by confronting him? Are you planning a biker gang standoff?"

The imagery in my head shows Jason and Marcus standing back-to-back and walking twenty paces, the winner being the fastest gunslinger in the ghetto. But this isn't like one of those old western movies that my dad likes to watch. This is real. I'm not even sure how bikers like to settle their disputes, but I can imagine it involves violence. I trust Jason.

God knows I do. But Marcus Jackal is a sly dog from what I've heard. He'll probably take a cheap shot at Jason or have someone on standby to shoot him in the back.

Jason sighs with resignation. "Stop trying to guess. If I tell you what's going down, it could blow everything. The less you know, the better."

I lean up to give him the stink-eye. "Jason, this is not okay. Stop treating me like I'm Bodie's little sister and start respecting me as your partner. I want to know because I care what happens to you."

Jason slips his hand beneath my nightdress and walks his fingers along my thigh. "And I care 'bout what happens to you too. For the record, I've never looked at you like Bodie's kid sister," he rasps, making me tingle in all the right places. Jason turns to get a better angle, his hot breath tickling my neck as his fingers reach my slit. "I've always had my eye on you ever since you flashed that big juicy peach at me in your gym skirt."

"I thought you said I had a fat ass," I grumble, even though what he's doing feels so good.

"I said it was like a big, ripe, juicy peach," Jason clarifies. "I couldn't exactly say I wanted to bite it in front of Bodie now, could I?"

I huff a lazy smile. "What else are you supposed to

do with peaches? You're supposed to bite right into them."

"That's easy. You're supposed to enjoy how goddamn juicy they are and savor the fuck out of them," Jason replies, his octave dropping to a sensual husk, brushing his lips against my skin, the vibration of his voice humming against me.

Jason is using seduction as a distraction tactic, but if he thinks I'll abandon my quest for answers, he's dead wrong. It just means I'll take whatever he gives me like the greedy girl I am, and then we'll resume our talk later. This little stunt is only delaying the inevitable. He'll come to learn that about me. One way or another, I always get my way.

"Hm, I prefer grapes over peaches. Same with plums. I always hate how messy they are," I say, my voice fragile and breathy as Jason strokes between my folds, plunging a finger inside my pussy. "The way the juice rolls down my chin." He drags a drenched digit through my slit and starts rimming my pebbled nub. "Then drips onto my chest, running straight between my tits and then soaking into my bra."

Jason chuffs a soft laugh. "That's the best part, making a mess and slurping those juices, then cleaning the droplets with my tongue." His strokes send sparks to my pleasure receptors, making my stomach muscles clench.

"Uh, Jason," I moan, and his face scrunches as if in pain, loving the sound of his name on my lips. "Someone might walk in." I tip my head back as my orgasm hits like an earthquake.

"That's it, baby. Let go," Jason groans. "If the doctor walks in right now and sees your cum face, he'd leave the room iron hard." He removes his soaked finger, then gets off the bed, moving into position so he can bury his face between my legs. I'm so unprepared for it. Still so touch-sensitive. I give a strangled squeak as Jason tongues my clit, the soft, textured heat dances around my pulsing nub, skilled, and tactile, leaving me gasping for breath, thighs trembling before another frisson of ecstasy shatters through me and wrings me out.

"Uh," I gasp loud enough to raise suspicion, the lights flickering behind my eyelids.

Jason tongues me until I can't take anymore, then wipes his mouth against my inner thighs. I hear the creak of his zipper and the rustle of denim. He crawls over me, covering me with his heft, then plunges his pierced appendage straight to the root. My pussy sucks down the entirety of his length, creating a vacuum of suction as Jason thrusts. We're half-clothed, and if anyone were to walk in here, they'd get a vulgar view. The bed creaks as Jason rocks against me, his bare ass grinding against my groin, his spread legs keeping mine wide open to accommodate him.

"Fuck, you got me," Jason groans into my ear. "I'm gonna cum." His face scrunches with pleasure, and he thrusts harder as he cums.

For a long while, I forget everything else and enjoy the safety of being wrapped in Jason's arms. It feels like I've rested my eyes for five minutes, but as I wake with a jolt, I can tell by looking through the window at the inky night sky that it's much later than I thought. Jason is gone. My mind fills with panic, and I grab my phone from the nightstand. With trembling hands, I drag my finger around the home screen, drawing the security pattern that unlocks the device, then accidentally tap an app. My family tracker app that Bodie set up for me. I'm about to close it, but something weird catches my eye, and it's enough for me to rub the sleep from my eyes and look closer.

"It can't be?" I utter bemusedly, seeing my brother's location marker moving toward the old container units behind the industrial park.

But it is. I see it clear as day. It's telling me that Bodie is here at Mountview and not sitting on a cloud wearing a toga, a fluffy pair of angel wings, and playing a golden harp, with a halo on his head.

"No, stupid." I tap the palm of my hand against my forehead. "He's dead. Someone has his phone."

I mull it over for all of two minutes before swinging my legs out of bed and snatching up the bag of clothes. My gut instinct is telling me that's where Jason is heading. I know it's stupid, but I can't just sit here and wait. I'll never forgive myself if something happens to Jason and I could have done something to stop it. So, I sneak out of the hospital, which isn't easy. It's miles away in the wrong direction. The only way for me to get there is if I hitch a ride or take the bus. Hitch-hiking is sketchy. Even in an emergency. The busses will take all fucking night to get there. But then I see a nurse get out of a cab, so I rush to catch the driver before he goes through the barrier. He agrees to take me most of the way, which is fine. It leaves a five-minute walk. It's nothing I can't handle. I'll be able to navigate my way around using the tracker app. It's a small price to pay for the truth.

CHAPTER NINE

I'm so hyped with adrenaline. My heart is beating so fast I can hear the blood pounding in my ears. Soapbox packed me some comfortable clothes and a pair of sneakers, which makes it easier to sneak up on Jason in stealth mode. I follow the location marker, glancing at my phone screen now and then to see which way it's moving. The industrial park is quiet at night, amplifying the slightest sound. I'm careful not to scrape my feet as I hasten my steps, taking care not to step on anything that'll give me away. Checking my phone, I can see the location marker has stopped behind an auto parts warehouse. The muffled voices coming from near the loading bay tell me that my suspicions are correct. Someone has Bodie's phone, or my brother has miraculously risen from the dead. The sickening thing is, I don't know what the fuck to expect, and it scares me.

"I knew you were working for Mayor Booker, just admit it!" I hear Jason shout, and my stomach lurches.

I turn off the app and keep hold of my phone in case I need to call Sheriff Dan for help. Now I have the gut-wrenching task of looking around the corner, dreading what I'll find. My head is screaming at me to run, but my heart refuses to listen. I need to know. So, I inhale a shaky breath and peek around the corner, seeing several dark figures standing parallel to one another in the floodlit loading yard. I recognize Mohawk Guy and his goons from the dive bar. There's another guy standing between them, and I wrack my brains to think where the hell I've seen him before. Then it hits me. It was the time the Jackals came to the auto shop and threatened Bodie. Holy shit, that's him. That must be Marcus Jackal. And Jason is practically within punching distance from him, with four guys I recognize from the back. Tex. Rooster. Hustle. *And wait.* I squint to get a better look. *That's the mysterious biker guy who saved me from the fire.* He's wearing the same biker leathers that have vertical red and white stripes down the sides of his suit. Then he turns to spit on the ground, and the side of his face is illuminated with light, confirming my thoughts.

"Oh my god," I utter; my heart shatters into a million pieces as my back slams against the wall.

Bodie is alive. They fucking lied to me. They all did.

"Sorry, can you repeat that?" Siri chimes through my phone, I'm holding onto it so tight.

I didn't realize I must have hit the button, and it picked up the sound of my voice. My eyes widen with terror, and I momentarily freeze with panic.

"Did you hear that?" a guy says in a gruff voice. "They're not alone. We're being set up."

Shit.

I hear the words, "Go check!" and my mind whirls into a frenzy. A fight breaks out between the gangs. That's when I start running, but I don't get far before someone grabs me by the hair and pulls me back, sending hellfire through my scalp. I go to scream, but then a rough hand clamps down over my mouth.

"What do we have here? Nosey little bitch, aren't you?" The guy rasps harshly against my ear. He shoves a gun against my back. "Start walking."

He keeps me at gunpoint as he takes me to the scene of the brawl, then raises his gun and fires a single shot into the sky to grab everyone's attention.

"Look what I found skulking around in the dark. Does this fine piece of ass belong to anyone?" he asks, and I figure he must be Mr. Mohawk because he's the only one missing from the fight.

I don't know if he remembers seeing me at the bar, but I'm hoping he doesn't. A surge of pure fear flashes through Bodie's eyes as he sees me, but he recovers quickly. The Hawks don't react to seeing me, and the worst thing of all nor does Jason.

"She's not with us," Jason answers impassively.

Marcus curls his hand to Mr. Mohawk as a gesture to hand me over. I get shoved toward Marcus who grabs me roughly by the jaw.

"Who are you, and why were you spying on us?" Marcus demands.

"Leave her be," Jason mutters in a bored tone, sounding like he couldn't give a fuck whether or not I live or die. And that hurts. It really fucking hurts to see him barely even bother to look at me. "She's probably just some junkie out to score. Stop stalling for time. We've got unfinished business."

Marcus's eyes narrow on me as if he's considering something. "You're right," he replies, tone empty, his eyes emotionless. He lets go of my jaw and then delivers a blinding back-handed slap that knocks me to the ground. My phone flies out of my hand and lands way out of reach.

I don't see how the Hawks react, but I hear the

click of a gun and know that I have about five seconds to live. Is this how it ends, with my brains splattered all over the asphalt? I squeeze my eyes shut as the resounding blast shatters through the sky. Only to find I can open them. The ground vibrates with a thundering of heavy footsteps, then I see blue flickering lights. A high-pitched noise screams through my head from the aftermath of the blast, and I can't make out what all the yelling is about until I see a hunched figure slumped on his knees, clutching his chest. I'm too shocked to take in all that's happening. I hear gunshots. The cops are here, and the Jackals ride away in a cloud of exhaust fumes. It's like time slows down all around me, and one minute I'm almost dead, then the next, I'm staring death straight in the face. Only I'm not the one who's dying.

"Jason!" I blurt out, then clamber toward him.

There's too much blood, and I cover his hands where he's pressing against the wound to stem the flow. He looks at me and manages a strained smile, and for the first time since leaving the hospital, he looks genuinely glad to see me. It was all an act. He does care. That doesn't excuse the fact that he lied.

"You just blew our entire operation," Sheriff Dan grumbles at me. "Months of work just got flushed down the toilet."

The Hawks don't seem so happy to see me. In fact, they're scowling at me like I just canceled Christmas. Sheriff Dan corrals me into the back of his car and drives me back to the hospital. Bodie rides in the ambulance with Jason, and the Hawks go home to their women as if nothing has happened. Now I know what Ivy meant when she tried to warn me about being kept in the dark. There's an ugly side to being a biker's chic. To them, we're nothing but property.

CHAPTER TEN

During the ride back to the hospital, I replay everything over in my head. I'm angry. I'm hurt. And now I don't know if there's anyone left to trust. What will our parents say when they find out about this? Do they know? Am I the only one who doesn't? I wonder if Ivy has been going through the same hellish torment, and if she has, then that sucks.

"You're going the wrong way to the hospital," I complain to Sheriff Dan.

He flicks his eyes at me in the interior mirror and huffs. "We're taking the scenic route. You should be glad I'm not throwing you in a cell for what you did." We take a sharp left, circling the outskirts of town. "If you must know, I'm giving you a way out. I told Bodie you would be better off going to the coast with your parents, but he assured me he'd keep an eye on you no matter what."

"He was the one who pulled me out of the fire," I reply.

"That's right," Dan confirmed. "And he's been keeping tabs on you the whole time he's been gone."

"Whose idea was it to pretend he was dead?" I interject.

Dan exhales a heavy sigh. "That was down to me. I asked Jason to keep tabs on you too, and look what happened there. You caused a scene, which forced him to take extreme measures to keep you safe. You're a walking liability."

His stern words held true, but it didn't mean I had to like them. The things he was saying to me left a bitter aftertaste.

"Are you saying Jason claimed me because he had to and not because he wanted to? But that's not what he told me," I challenge.

Eventually, we approach the hospital parking lot, and Dan swings the car toward the barrier a little too forcefully. "Do you believe everything people tell you?" His cynical tone hits me like a slap across the face. "You were told what you needed to hear. And if you have any sense, you'll pack a bag and get the fuck out of Mountview because like it or not, you have a target on your back. I imagine Booker will have heard all about our big fuck-up and will send his goons after anyone connected to Jason. I've got to get home to check on Liv; although I doubt Booker will harm a hair on her head. He's still sweet on her after all these years." There's resentment in Dan's voice as if those words are laced with poison.

He stops the patrol car and pulls the handbrake sharply. "Go, get out." He jerks his head at the door. "Get checked over, then get the fuck out of town. I better not see you after tonight."

"Not before you tell me about Booker and Jason's mom," I demand, grating on Dan's last nerve.

Dan scowls at me. "I thought she cheated on me with him back when we were teens. It took a while for us to move past it, and when we did, several years had passed." He taps the steering wheel with his forefinger, considering whether to continue. "Look, for what it's worth, I'm sorry how things turned out. I love Jason like he was my own flesh and blood, but this is something you don't wanna be mixed up in. Take my advice and get the hell out of Mountview tonight if you can. Don't wait. Just go. I'd hate to have to bury one of Garrett Blake's kids for real. Your father and I go way back. He's one of the good guys. It would do him a world of good if you spent some time with him for a while. Go fill your lungs with some clean sea air and wait for the dust to settle." Dan hands back my scuffed phone. "An officer found this. I figured you'd need it."

I reach out to take it, curling my fingers around it. "Thanks. But what about Bodie and Jason?"

Dan's brows dimple in the middle. "I know you're mad. You have every right to be. But please believe me when I tell you they were acting on my command. I've been trying to take down Booker for a very long time. I've spent my career trying to bring him down. Just know, they didn't mean for you to get caught in the middle of this. It's not the way it was supposed to be."

I nod to show I understand, even though it's not completely true. I doubt I'll ever fully understand their reasons. There's never a good reason to lie to the ones you love. Without trust, there's nothing. And right now, I have zero trust to go around. I'm all out. It's over. I want to say it was good while it lasted, but that would be lying. Nothing was real. It was all based on lies. Now I know what Dan is asking me to do, and it makes sense. I should go. There's nothing left for me here, just a burned-down auto shop and a house filled with painful memories.

"I should probably go say goodbye," I say, my voice cracking with emotion.

Dan flashes a sympathetic smile as I leave. He

doesn't wait around. He's already driving away as the sliding glass doors open, and the building swallows me whole. I tell the nurse on the reception desk that I'm Jason Knight's girlfriend. She tells me he's been rushed into surgery, and that I can wait in the family room with his brother. *Brother. That's rich.* Blinking back the tears in my eyes, I follow the signs along the corridor until I find the right room. Then as I go inside, I'm confronted by Bodie. He stands quickly and rushes to hug me, but I recoil from his touch as if it repulses me. I should be relieved to see him standing there alive and well with nothing but superficial bruises from the fight. But I'm not. I'm angry. No, I'm more than that. I'm broken. I feel betrayed. And nothing anyone can say will ever make this okay.

"I fucking mourned you," I spit out the words through gulping breaths, trying to keep the rising bile from creeping up my throat. "How dare you try to comfort me now. Where the fuck have you been all this time?" I knock his hand away as he reaches out to touch me.

Bodie flinches with regret. "I've been staying with Dan and Liv."

I place my hand over my stomach and take a step back. "I don't believe this. Liv is Mom's friend. She held onto our mother as she sobbed at your graveside. I can believe this from Dan, but her?" I stagger back and collapse onto the sofa, then lean forward to rest my head in my hands, driving my fingers through my hair. "How could you do this to her . . . to Dad . . . and to Ivy?"

Bodie grips the bridge of his nose and grimaces. "I'm going to explain everything after we stop Booker. This is bigger than us, Kiera. It's bigger than you know."

"Your girlfriend is heavily pregnant," I say, my face twisting with contempt. "When were you gonna come clean about that?"

"I wanted to," Bodie replies, rubbing the back of his neck. "But I knew Mom would never leave town if she knew."

So, he was planning to wait until Dan nailed Booker and then miraculously resurrect from the dead. "You're not Jesus, Bodie. I for one won't blame Ivy if she kicks your ass to the curb. You're an asshole," I yell at him. Then point aimlessly at the wall, not really knowing where the surgery room is. "And Jason is an asshole too. As far as I'm concerned, you can both screw yourselves. I'm out of here. I'm done. You've got what you wanted. I'll move in with Mom and Dad and be out of your hair for good."

"Keira," Bodie says my name pleadingly.

I pause at the door, then slowly turn my head. "I'm glad you're not dead, but don't ever pretend to care because this only proves that you don't."

Bodie sighs sadly as I leave. If all he can say is how he did it for justice, then I don't want to hear it. I would have understood that. I wouldn't have tried to talk him out of it. Our parents wouldn't have breathed a word of it to anyone. We've always handled things as a family. So, why does it feel like Bodie's loyalty to his brotherhood – the fucking Knight Hawks – came first before anything else? This only proves that I'm not cut out to be a biker's girlfriend. I don't want to be second best. I'm an all or nothing kind of girl.

Jason's surgery goes well. He was lucky. The bullet missed his vital organs. The fucker will live to ride another day. Is this relief I'm feeling? Maybe. It's the same relief I felt when I saw Bodie was okay. But there's no way they're getting let off the hook that easily. They hurt me. I want them to suffer. Jason is awake when the nurse brings me to his room. The word has gotten around the hospital that their missing patient has returned, and my doctor isn't too impressed with me. Jason and Bodie don't know this, but he signed my discharge notes while I've been waiting. I'm thinking about taking Dan's advice. I'm here to say goodbye.

"Hey, beautiful," Jason slurs his words. "Come over here and let me take a look at you."

I sit on the side of his bed, and Jason's eyes twitch questioningly. "What's wrong?" he asks.

"You knew about Bodie all along, didn't you?" I say accusingly.

I can tell by the way he cringes that he's sorry I had to find out this way.

"Did Sheriff Dan tell you to claim me?" I swallow the lump in my throat.

Silence.

I force myself to look at Jason and see his eyes drowning in anguish.

"Don't make me repeat the question," I say, my voice wispy and frail.

Jason's hand curls around my wrist gently. I don't pull away from him. I maintain eye contact as I wait.

"Yeah, but—" he stammers to explain, but I stand, having just had my worst fear confirmed.

"So, that's it. I was just a loose end you needed to tie up." I put on my bravest face as I look at him, my expression hard as stone. "Well, now that's out there, you don't need to pretend anymore. Good luck taking down Booker. Maybe I'll see you around if I ever come back to visit."

I watch the color drain from Jason's face. It's like

he's too stunned to speak, my words knocking the wind right out of him. He makes to move, but then collapses back onto the bed and grimaces with pain, his hand flying up to cover the freshly taped gauze on his chest. I feel a stab of guilt as I leave the room, but it's quickly forgotten as I walk down the corridor. I wasn't too harsh. My reaction is justified. I'm too busy mulling things over in my head when somebody pulls me into a dark room and insists that I hush.

"It's me." I recognize Bodie's hushed murmur. "Don't make a sound. He's here."

"Who's here?" I whisper.

"Booker," Bodie replies. "Look." He jerks his head at the slit of glass in the door, and we both peer through it and see Mayor Booker storming down the hall with Marcus Jackal three steps behind him.

I blink hard, my heart thumping with alarm as they both enter Jason's room.

"What do we do? They're going in there to finish the job!" I say, panicking.

"No, they're not. Let's see if we can listen." Bodie leads the way as we sneak across the corridor to eavesdrop on them.

"What do I fuckin' owe the pleasure?" I hear Jason crudely say.

"Can't a father come and visit his son in the hospital?" Mayor Booker replies, making my eyes bulge with that revelation.

I hear Jason snort with amusement. "You have some nerve. I'll give you that. What the fuck is he doing here? Get him out of my face."

"Can't you boys just learn to get along?" Booker tries to sound all paternal as he castigates them. "If you want to behave like children, I'll treat you like children. Marcus, say sorry to your little brother for shooting him in the chest."

Brother!

Bodie sees my alarm and waves his hand to silence me. He puts his finger against his lips, his frown deepening.

"I wasn't aiming at him. That stupid dick jumped in the way to save some crack whore from getting her brains blown out," Marcus protests.

Jason saved me. He took a bullet in the chest and could have been killed instead of letting Marcus shoot me.

"I'll fucking kill you!" Jason roars, and I'm shocked to hear Jason get triggered as Marcus talks shit about me.

"Ah, how gallant. Jumping to your girlfriend's defense," Marcus taunts Jason. "I know who she is. I remembered where I'd seen her before. She's that grease monkey from the garage. The one you allegedly claimed in the dive bar. I'm surprised she made it out of the inferno alive. What is it with these Blake kids? They have a habit of coming back from the dead."

"Stay the fuck away from them, or I swear I'll kill you," Jason vows, and it takes all my restraint not to go barging in and jump to his defense because hell knows I want to.

Now I understand why Jason and Bodie didn't want to tell me everything. It's because Booker is Jason's real father. And I have a gut feeling that Liv didn't cheat on Dan from what I can tell by Jason's resentment. Bodie drags me back inside the empty room just as Booker and Marcus barge out through the door. Booker looks stressed. He turns on Marcus and grabs the front of his T-shirt, his face reddening with anger.

"If you've screwed things up for me, we're through," Booker growls vehemently. "I said I wanted you to break him, so do it. You know his weakness. Find her and end this."

CHAPTER ELEVEN

Bodie is left shaking with anger as they leave. It feels weird to be at the top of a biker thug's hit list. I should be scared shitless. There isn't a funny side. So why does it amuse me? I can't help but chuckle at the irony. After all, Jason claimed me to save me. So far, his plan has fallen flat on its ass. I'm in danger now more than ever. Marcus thinks he can hurt Jason by hurting me. So, by claiming me, Jason put a bigger target on my head.

"The Jackal shot Jason, and now he's threatening to kill you," Bodie utters disdainfully. "As our queen, what are your orders?"

I double-take, scrunching my face with incredulity. "Are you serious? *Now* you want my input?"

"Hey, I did what I thought was right." Bodie holds

his hands up defensively. "I'm not saying it was the right move. But I thought it was at the time. Now I'm admitting I was wrong. We all were. I can spend the rest of my life on my knees begging for forgiveness, but that won't change what's happening now. I'm on your side, Kiera. Whatever you want to do, I'll back you up one hundred percent. In fact, I'll prove it to you."

Bodie pulls me by the arm, and I go with him into Jason's recovery room where we find him fully dressed and ready to walk out of there without telling anybody. I have no room to talk, having done the exact same thing tonight, but Jason was shot. My injuries are mild compared to his.

"Hey, what the hell are you doing?" I say reflexively. "You should be resting. Get back in bed."

Jason is shocked to see me, and his expression melts with relief. "Keira. You didn't leave. What made you come back?"

I throw Bodie the stink-eye and fold my arms across my chest. "It seems you idiots can't cope without me, so . . ." I bounce my shoulders, pretending not to give a fuck. But that's not true. I do care. If I didn't, I wouldn't be here.

Jason clears the space between us, then pulls me against him, wincing gingerly from the pain. "It wasn't all lies, Peaches. When I told you I loved you, I meant it." Jason holds my face between his warm hands and looks down into my eyes. "I love you so much I'd die for you."

I can feel Bodie shrinking away with awkwardness, not wanting to witness a tender moment between his best friend and his sister. And as much as I've longed to hear Jason say this, because it never gets old, I'm still angry. I'm upset they didn't trust me enough to include me in their plans in the first place. Now it's my turn to lay down the rules. No more secrets and lies. If they want my forgiveness, we wipe the slate clean and start again. This time, with rules that respect everyone. The brotherhood and the sisterhood included. We're not just brainless accessories they can dangle from their arms and ride pillion around town, bang whenever they want, however they choose, never to complain, talk back, or have an opinion. I'll tell the girls the same thing next time I see them. It's time to make a stand.

"Jason, Havoc, or whatever you prefer me to call you in front of witnesses. I love you too. But you're still an asshole. You broke my trust, and I think you should be punished before you're forgiven. Bodie too, but I'll let Ivy deal with him." I smile maliciously, catching the flicker of approval in Jason's eyes.

"Kiera ought to have a say in how we handle both Marcus and Booker," Bodie says, sticking up for me.

"None of this would have happened if we had told her everything from the start."

"You're right," Jason replies, flicking his gaze from Bodie and back at me. "It's my fault for making the wrong call. When all this is done, I'll get on my knees and kiss your ass. Anywhere you want."

"Well, that's a nauseating thought," Bodie mutters behind me. "I'll send word to Rooster and tell him to bring the truck." Bodie steps outside to make the call, leaving Jason and me alone.

"I thought I lost you twice tonight," Jason mentions, stroking the sides of my face with his thumbs. "First when Marcus aimed that gun at your head, then when you tried to dump me just now."

I huff a sigh and blink. "Yeah, well, I'm still considering things," I reply. "You've got a lot of making up to do. You both have."

"How about right now?" Jason suggests, dipping down for a kiss. It's one I avoid, and he catches my cheek instead.

"Not so fast, Romeo. We've got unfinished business to do. I want to help." I meet Jason's gaze, and a moment of understanding settles between us.

"What do you have in mind?" Jason asks.

"Well, since I fucked up Dan's plan, I'm volunteering to offer myself up as bait," I mention, and Jason splutters.

"Fuck no," he blurts out, reacting exactly how I expect him to.

"Your dad wants me dead to break you, and Marcus resents you because you're better than him. I get there's sibling rivalry going on. Marcus seems jealous of you. It got me thinking that if I can prey on Marcus's ego and convince him I want payback for being used, he'll fall for it out of wanting to spite you. Then I can seduce him and get him to spill all his secrets about Booker," I explain, thinking I have a solid plan. However, Jason's outraged expression tells me otherwise.

Jason holds my lips together to stop me from talking, his unsettled frown deepening. "Firstly, Booker is not my dad and never will be. Dan is my dad in my heart." He taps his chest. "Secondly, Marcus is no brother of mine. And if you think for one second I'm just gonna stand back and let that bastard touch you, you're gravely mistaken, sweetheart."

I fling my hands up and step back. "Well, it's not as if we can break into Town Hall and scope out Booker's office, is it? If you want to nail Booker, we've got to get Marcus to spill his guts. He does all the donkey work. I bet it won't be too difficult to get him to talk. He looks like the type to brag."

This gives Jason something to think about. But the pregnant silence is broken when Jason's phone rings. He's quick to answer it.

"Dan, is everything okay?" He pauses to listen, his eyes widening with shock. "What? How do you know that?" His terrified eyes dart to me, and I know in my gut that something is wrong. "I'm on my way."

"What's going on?" I ask.

Jason shoves his arms through his leather jacket and puts away his phone. "Dan went home and found the front door had been kicked in. My mom is gone, but her car, purse, and phone are still there. Someone has taken her. It must have literally happened right before he got home because one of the neighbors heard screaming and saw a truck and several bikes speeding away. They were just about to call the cops when Dan arrived. It seems like Marcus doesn't trust Booker either. He's a loose cannon. He must get that from our sociopath father. I've got to find him and stop him before it's too late."

"Okay, so, where's their hideout?" I shrug.

Jason scrubs a hand over his face, frustratedly. "I don't know. It could be anywhere."

"It's a good thing you have me as bait then. Marcus

is going to come for me, and you're going to let him. I'll do my best to gain his trust, then you can track his ass back to his hideout," I say, putting it out there for him to consider.

A dark shadow crosses Jason's face, and he moves closer to stroke my face. "Okay. This one time, do what you gotta do, and we'll draw a line in the sand and forget about it. If he hurts you, I'll kill him."

He's just given me the green light to use my pussy as a decoy, which for any man is a hard pill to swallow.

"Marcus is the target. I'm yours," I remind him. "Only yours. Forever and always."

CHAPTER TWELVE

After bringing Bodie up to speed with the plan, I take a cab home. We thought it would be more believable if I stayed angry about Bodie and Jason's betrayal. I mean, I'm not just gonna let it slide. Of course, I'm angry, and rightly so. But I can appreciate why they did it. The cab driver drops me at the edge of my drive, and after paying him the fare, I fish my smashed phone and keys from my purse and practically run to the front door. This is a nice neighborhood. It's quiet throughout the day and night. Nothing remotely interesting happens here. If I scream, I can guarantee my neighbors will hear it. They are so nosey; they would come out to investigate. Hopefully, I won't need their help because the Hawks stashed a hidden camera inside the lining of my purse so they could see and hear everything I could. Hustle didn't make a clean job of it. He's no seamstress, and it's not exactly my best purse. It wasn't expensive. Like everything I own, it's a little rough around the edges. No one will suspect it's been tampered with, which is good, I guess. It means a dumb fuck like Marcus won't suspect anything. Even if he rummages through it and tips the contents out, he won't find it. I pretend I'm on a call to my mom, complaining about Jason being the biggest asshole on the face of the planet, telling no one whatsoever that I never want to ever lay eyes on Jason again. If Marcus is skulking around in the shadows, it'll pique his interest. He can't use me as a target if he thinks Jason and I have severed ties.

"The bastard was just using me as a smokescreen," I mutter, opening the door and sparing a wary glance around. "Yeah, I'll pack my things and leave this shit-hole for dust." I continue the fake conversation after I close the door on the off chance someone is listening. "Okay, I'll buy a train ticket and call you as soon as I get there. I love you. Bye."

"Going somewhere?" A deep rasp comes from the open sitting room doorway.

I recognize it immediately and stumble against the wall with fright. "Holy shit. How did you get in here?"

Marcus flicks on the light switch, flooding the

room with light that spills out into the hall. He must have come straight here to wait for me after sending his goons to go after Jason's mom, Liv.

Marcus casually leans against the doorframe, a cocky smirk scrawled halfway across his face. "I used the key beneath the doormat. Not bad for a crack whore," he mentions mockingly, his dark eyes fixated on me like a predator stalking his prey.

"I'm not on crack. And I don't appreciate being called a whore," I say, offended by his remark.

"You're fucking Havoc though," he replies crassly. "That tells me you don't have any standards."

He isn't handsome like Jason, but there's something dangerously sexy about his rugged looks that even I can't deny. Not that it's enough to turn my head to the dark side. But still. I'm only human. Marcus looks like the type of guy who could bend a woman across the kitchen table and make her forget her name. Jason may not like to hear it, but he and his half-brother are the same in that respect. I should be grateful I'm not dead already. Marcus isn't pointing a gun at me, but I can imagine he has one tucked inside the waistband of his jeans. I can see the way he brazenly checks me out, his eyes lingering too long on my heaving chest. Bastard or not, he's still a man.

"Yeah, and that's ten seconds of my life that I'm

never getting back. That fucker used me, and I used him," I retaliate, making Marcus raise his brows with interest. "I just wanted to find out what happened to my brother, but I guess the joke was on me because they're all a bunch of liars. You should have aimed a little higher and done us both a favor." It feels wrong to say all this about the man I love, but it's necessary to make my story believable. I know I have a vicious tongue and can say all sorts of hurtful things if I want to.

Marcus scrubs a hand over his face as he processes that. And judging by the look on his face, he's stumped by my revelation. This has thrown a spanner in the works. If I'm nothing to Jason, then I'm worthless to Marcus. Kiera – one. Marcus – a big fat zero.

"Oh, man. Who would have thought Havoc was a two-pump chump?" Marcus mutters, mulling that over. "I can't believe we're from the same gene pool."

I inwardly cringe at the thought of Jason sitting on the clubhouse couch between his snickering biker buddies, seething at me for trashing his performance. He'll punish me severely for this. I just know he will.

"Is that all you took from that?" I roll my eyes and bravely walk past him on my way to the kitchen.

Marcus doesn't grab me, but he's right behind me as I turn around. "Well, this changes things," he gruffs ominously. "I came here to leave a message to my enti-tled prick of a brother, which all seems pretty pointless now." I side-eye the knife rack and contemplate whether I could snatch the carving knife before he does. "But now you've seen me. I can't exactly let you go running to the cops."

I hold his gaze. "The same cops who covered up my brother's so-called death. Yeah, right."

Marcus's throat bobs as he swallows. "Still . . . you're a loose end."

I set my purse down and tilt the angle of the camera away, not wanting anyone to see what I do next. "You know Jason claimed me, don't you?"

Marcus furrows his brows in a humored frown. "And your point is?"

I step toward him and put my hands on his chest, playing the art of seduction to the best of my ability. "If you really want to ruin him, you could start with his reputation."

This has to work. I can't screw this up. Everything is riding on me gaining Marcus's trust. Liv Knight is fuck knows where, surrounded by filthy scumbags who could be doing fuck knows what to her. With any luck, Marcus will start thinking with his dick and be dumb enough to take me to her. I just need to grab my bag, and I'll be fine. Jason and Bodie will be able to find me.

Marcus doesn't flinch as I slide my palms around his shoulders, moving close enough to smell the tobacco on his breath. His eyes blaze into mine with a hint of distrust, the corners twitching a little like he's considering something. Not that it takes more than a second for him to decide what he wants as he reaches down to squeeze my ass, the pressure of his fingers digging a little too tight for my liking. Marcus delves right in for the kill, crudely kissing my neck and groping my breasts beneath my hoodie. It crawls my skin to let him touch me like this, but the more he thinks he'll get his dick wet, the less likely he'll want to kill me. If I want Marcus to trust me, I'll need to be smart.

I'm sorry, Jason. I'm doing this for you and your mom.

"Let's go upstairs," I utter before Marcus roughly kisses me, and I reciprocate.

Marcus swirls his tongue inside my mouth, hardly giving me a chance to breathe. He's rough and driven by something more than lust – a cold vendetta against Jason that seems to be fueled by jealousy. I let him wriggle a hand down my sweatpants and cop a feel of my pussy; even parting my legs so he can drag his finger through my slit.

"Here's fine," Marcus replies, proving my assumption about him right. "We don't have time for pillow talk. Turn around."

I'm glad that I angled the camera away because things are about to get ugly. Marcus yanks down my sweats, then forces me flat against the table, stuffing a dish towel in my mouth. I hear a rustle of denim, then he spits, slathers his saliva around my pussy, then drives his cock inside me and starts thrusting. A moment of confusion crashes over me as he humps away, puffing and panting with exertion. I want to ask if it's all the way in because it doesn't feel like it is. But before I can fathom whether this is a joke, Marcus barks out a harsh cry and starts shuddering behind me. Should I fake moaning or claw at the tabletop? I'm just slumped here as wooden as the furniture not knowing what the fuck to think. A strangled yelp lets me know he's finished, and I bite down on the dish towel to stop myself from laughing. If I didn't feel it, does it count?

I spit out the towel. "Oh my god," I rush my words to sound breathless. "That was amazing!" It's not about what I say, it's the way I say it. Jason knows me well enough to tell when I'm being sarcastic. Marcus doesn't. He tucks away his flaccid junk and buttons his jeans like he's God's gift, thinking he just rocked my world and not just my kitchen table. I use the dish towel to clean myself, then pull up my sweatpants, hoping I did enough to convince him.

"I can't wait to see the look on Havoc's face when I parade you around town. It'll ruin him." Marcus rubs his hands together gleefully. "Dear old Dad will fucking hate it. He wants you dead, but fuck him. This is my time to shine."

"Does this mean I can stay at your place?" I pretend to be so into Marcus I'm practically tripping over my tongue to kiss his ass. "If your dad wants me dead, there's no telling what he'll do."

"Makes sense to keep an eye on you," he replies, glancing around the kitchen. "I need people to see us together if this is going to work." Marcus jerks his head toward the door. "Get your things and let's go."

I grab my purse from the table, then grab a change of clothes, shoving everything into a backpack. This is it. I'm about to make another reckless move that could potentially get me killed, and it should scare me. Only it doesn't. It thrills me. The danger, adrenaline rush, and the thought of jumping into the midst of all the action turns me on more than anything. I was made for this life. I just didn't know it until I fell headfirst into a steaming pile of fuckery. Marcus beckons me to follow, then turns his back to walk through the hall. That's when I grab the biggest carving knife from the rack, wrap it in the cum-stained dishtowel, and quickly shove it in my backpack. I raise my purse up to my face and wink at the camera, letting the Hawks know the plan is working.

CHAPTER THIRTEEN

Marcus brings me to a crummy old farmhouse surrounded by woodland and is tucked away on the outskirts of town. My legs are shaking as I get off the back of his motorcycle. I do well to walk up the weathered wooden steps on trembling legs, ignoring the leering stares and heckling from the Jackals. There are empty beer bottles everywhere I look, crumpled cigarette packets, and discarded takeout containers. I thought the Hawks were messy, but these guys are pure slobs.

"Whatcha got there, boss?" Mr. Mohawk drawls in a lazy tone. "Is that the same chic from last night?"

"The very same," Marcus confirms. "She's Havoc's ex old lady."

Mr. Mohawk gawks at me, then his eyes widen

with realization. "Oh, shit. I know where I've seen you before. You're the chic from the bar. The one Havoc banged in the manager's office."

"We didn't bang," I'm quick to clarify. "He smacked me around for talking back to him."

The Jackals chortle, mostly finding my outburst funny. They flick their attention between Marcus and me as if they are waiting for him to slap me for speaking out of turn.

"Women should be seen and not heard," Marcus remarks, jabbing his finger at me. "Now, get in there and grab a broom. I want this shithole spick and span before the sun comes up, or the next fucking you get will be my fist up your ass." He waits until I scurry past and then forcibly smacks my butt enough to make it sting.

Holding my purse strap tightly, I pretend to look around the rickety porch to give the Hawks a rough estimate of how many Jackals they're dealing with. Marcus wastes no time in telling his goons all about us bumping uglies, embellishing the truth to make several seconds stretch to half an hour. While his buddies are patting his back for being such a wild stallion, I hurry inside to look for Liv. Even if I was gonna spend the night cleaning, it would take more than one night to get this place spotless. The very air I breathe is ninety-nine percent stale piss and cigarette smoke. I wouldn't let my dog sleep in here if I owned one. Fuck knows how the Jackals can stand it. Maybe they're nose blind.

Covering my airways with the neckline of my hoodie, I breathe my warm scent as I scour the house, kicking aside all the trash. There's a ratty couch in the sitting room, a decent flatscreen TV in one corner, and a small veneer table with a stack of playing cards on it. I'm not sure if the previous owner nailed planks of wood to cover the windows or if the Jackals did it. I go upstairs, taking each pitted step one at a time, not knowing what I might find up there. It's just as I thought; it's dingy, but less cluttered than downstairs. I expect to find bare mattresses on the floor, not mismatched single beds. They all appear to sleep in one room with their dirty laundry piled high on the landing. I can see the bathroom through an open doorway, and next to it there's a locked door with a key protruding from the lock.

An ear-splitting whistle makes me almost jump out of my skin. "Woman, where'd you go?" Marcus calls out from downstairs.

Retracting my hand from the key, I abandon the search temporarily and go back downstairs to see what he wants.

"I was just looking around," I say, keeping a casual tone. "And for the record, my name is Keira."

"I'm not interested in learning your name. I'm only keeping you around because you put out. There's a roll of trash bags in the kitchen," Marcus mentions, pointing the way. "Don't fucking let me catch you going upstairs unsupervised."

"Not even to use the bathroom?" I answer back, much to Marcus's annoyance.

Marcus eyes me distrustfully. "Can't have you snooping around places you've got no business to snoop or hopping from dick to dick. If you know what's good for you, you'll keep that pussy contained. If I want you to blow me, you'll get on your knees and do it. If I tell you to drop your panties and bend the fuck over, you'll fucking do it. Do you hear me?"

"Loud and clear," I grumble.

Marcus observes me for a long moment, probably wondering what I'm thinking and wishing he could read minds.

"You're not scared of me, are you?" he asks, his eyes narrowing.

I snap right back into acting, pretending to be into him. "Should I be?" I come closer to him and snake my arms around his waist.

Marcus doesn't move a muscle; he just lets me rub

against him like a bitch in heat. "Fuck me over and you'll regret it," he warns.

"Speaking of fucking over," I begin, getting ready to drop the Booker bomb. "Won't Booker be mad about you keeping me around?"

Marcus snorts. "That bastard is using me to do his dirty work. He tracked me down, offered me a job, and I just about snatched his hand off at the offer. He wanted me to drive some people off their land; either they sold to the developers, or we'd run them out of town. I was promised it would be fifty-fifty, but so far, Booker has fallen short of his end of the bargain. Can't say I'm surprised."

"Oh, why's that?" I ask, stepping back to film his revelation.

"Because the dude is a serial rapist who goes around roofying women to get his dick wet. That's what he does. One minute he's talking to a woman at a bar, and the next he's slipping a little something extra into their drink when they're not looking. The next thing they know, they wake up naked in some dingy motel with no memory of what happened the night before. I'm a product of Booker's dick-happy antics, and so is Havoc. And there's plenty more where we came from. His out of court settlement bill is enough to make a man's dick stay limp indefinitely. Eventually, they all creep out of the woodwork, and his lawyers pay them off and make them sign a non-disclosure order. The only woman to never ask for a cent is Havoc's mom. According to Booker, they have history. He's head over heels for the bitch, and I can't say I blame him. She's a knockout."

Marcus isn't shy with the details. It seems he doesn't care what happens to Booker as long as Marcus gets his money.

"Liv hates Booker," I mention.

Marcus tilts his head to one side. "Yeah, so I believe." He silently analyzes me for a moment, then his eyes harden. "The boys paid her a visit tonight. My orders." He studies my reaction, which I don't give because I know what he's doing, and I'm not falling for it. "They took turns on her, fucking her up real good."

I swallow my revulsion, hoping it doesn't show. "Then what?"

Marcus shrugs. "They brought her here."

"What are you going to do to her?" I remain as calm as I possibly can.

"She's leverage in case Booker tries to stitch me up," Marcus replies, jerking his head to the stairs. "Why don't we go upstairs and say hi?"

"THIS IS THE POLICE. COME OUT WITH

YOUR HANDS UP. WE HAVE YOU SURROUNDED." Sheriff Dan's voice echoes from a speakerphone.

Marcus blanches with panic, then joins his goons as they rush to peer through the barricaded windows. I don't hang around to be used as a body shield. I run upstairs, unlock the door, and find a petrified Liv gagged and bound to a chair. She panics at first. Then as her eyes settle on me, I see them crease with relief. She sobs loudly as I take the knife from my bag and use it to cut her loose. I tug the knot to remove the gag, and Liv spits it out, reaching out to hug me.

"Keira, thank God," Liv wails. "They said Jason and Dan were dead."

I shake my head. "No, they lied. They're both fine. They're coming to save us."

Liv gasps a ragged sob. "They hurt me. They hurt me like he did. Did they hurt you too?"

I hug her tight, and my heart sinks with sympathy. "No, I let Marcus touch me so he would bring me to you." I lean back and hold her puffy, tear-streaked face. "Don't worry, Liv. We'll make them pay. Booker too. But first, we've gotta get out of here."

All that follows is the rapid sound of gunfire. There's a warzone down there, and I'm not sure whose side is winning. Liv and I huddle together, both watching the door, afraid to see the wrong guy walk through it. It feels like a lifetime, but when the noise eventually settles and we hear heavy footsteps coming upstairs, I adjust my grip on the knife. I'm ready to kill to protect us. It's either them or us. And I'm not afraid to follow through with it.

CHAPTER FOURTEEN

Nothing was stopping me from looking through the window to see who was winning or poking my head around the door to listen to what was going on. But in the heat of the moment, fear rooted me to the spot. Liv clings to me as the door flies open, and we see a tall figure standing in the doorway.

"Mom, Keira!"

It's Jason. We're fast on our feet to run to him, and as he throws his arms around us, the knife slips from my hand and clatters on the floor.

"It's okay, they can't hurt you anymore," he says, which sounds a lot like they won't be hurting anyone ever.

I don't care. I'm just glad it's over.

"Liv," Dan calls out, and Liv dashes to meet him.

Jason's hands fly to my face, his thumbs sweeping away my tears. "You did good. I'm so proud of you," he reassures me.

"I'm so sorry," I reply, meaning it.

"Those memories die tonight," Jason reminds me of our deal. "You did what you had to. I never want to speak of it again. We're going home with a clean slate."

I know it's what we agreed, but it still sickens me to think of Marcus getting his rocks off inside me – barely inside me. All he did was tickle my hole with his pin dick and leave a gross, sticky mess inside my panties.

"Is he dead?" I ask, searching Jason's gaze.

"No, but he won't be walking for a while," Jason answers bluntly. "Thought you might have jumped into the thick of the fight and I'd need to save your peachy ass again."

"I might be a lot of things, but I'm not stupid enough to bring a knife to a gunfight," I mention humorously.

Jason's eyes warm with mirth. "Let's get you home."

"Whose home?" I reply, shuddering at the thought of seeing my kitchen table again.

"Ours," he clarifies.

"What about Booker?" I arch a quizzical eyebrow.

Jason's smirk says it all. They've got it covered. "Thanks to you we've got a confession from Marcus. And when my mom testifies, no one will ever believe Booker again. I've agreed to take a DNA test. And I'm happy to tell the court all about Booker's bribery."

Jason picks up the kitchen knife and my bag, then we go outside to see the aftermath of the shootout. Marcus is being driven away in the back of a cop car, the same as the few remaining Jackals. The unfortunate few are being bagged and tagged and shoved into a coroner's van. Liv waves at me from the passenger seat of Dan's police car, and he mentions to Jason that they'll be staying at his apartment until the forensic team is done taking DNA evidence from Liv's place. The Hawks gather around us, but instead of judgmental eyes, they regard me with awe. It seems I've taken one for the team, and now I'm one of them – a full-fledged member of the crew.

This time, when I go to the clubhouse, I don't feel like an outsider. I'm part of the family. It feels good knowing I have the Knight Hawks seal of approval. I can move on from tonight and leave all the bad shit behind me.

A line in the sand.

A clean slate.

But it seems that I've spoken too soon because we've

just left one warzone and stepped into another. Bodie walks through the door first, and Ivy does not seem impressed. She spits out a mouthful of orange juice with shock, then sends the glass hurtling toward Bodie.

Okay, so this confirms the Hawks didn't go home. They must have been watching the live recording from Dan's office.

"You bastard! I thought you were dead," Ivy screams like a banshee.

Bodie dodges the glass, and it shatters against the wall, splattering shards of glass and juice everywhere. Tex whistles at Dude and takes him outside to do his business. The poor dog doesn't know what's going on. Out of everyone, he's just ecstatic to see Bodie.

Jason pulls me out of the way, and the Hawks and their women all run for cover. We seek sanctuary in the kitchen area as Ivy stalks toward Bodie.

"I'm gonna kill you for real," Ivy threatens.

Bodie holds up his hands, his eyes widening. "Just hear me out."

A dull thud followed by Bodie making an "Oof" sound lets me know Ivy just kneed him where the sun doesn't shine. I probably shouldn't laugh, but it's funny as fuck, and I can't help it.

Soapbox grins, unable to help herself from looking

over. "I give them two minutes and then they'll be fucking." She catches my eye and shrugs. "It's their dynamic. You'll get used to it."

And she isn't wrong. The fighting stops, and the kissing sounds start, and that's when everyone turns around and pretends the gasping grunting noises aren't really happening. I guess I shouldn't be shocked. It is a biker gang. Anything goes. Soapbox sweeps away the broken glass so that Tex can bring Dude back inside.

"Can we join them?" Tequila asks Hustle, shaking his arm. "They're really getting into it."

Hustle wrinkles his nose disapprovingly. "Nah, give them some space to make up."

Tequila pouts. "Spoilsport."

Claws rolls her eyes and sighs. "Ugh, quit sulking and maybe I'll let you tag-team with us later," she mentions, getting a nod of approval from Tex.

I turn to Jason and notice him smirking, probably wondering what I make of all this. This will take some getting used to, but the way they talk about sharing makes it seem like harmless fun.

"Listen up," Jason announces, getting everyone's attention. Everyone except Bodie and Ivy who are busy banging away on the couch. "Keira has proven her loyalty to the club, and tonight will be her initiation ceremony."

My eyes bulge. "What do you mean?"

The women rally around with excitement as I wonder what a biker initiation entails. I'm a dab hand at shooting pool. I know how to hustle a poker game. And I can drink like a fish, but I hate beer—anything but beer. *Ugh, God. What will they throw at me?*

"It's been so long since we held a good biker rut around here. The last rut was Bodie's, and Stiletto struggled to sit for a week," Soapbox says excitedly.

I feel myself shrink to the floor like a mouse. "What the fuck is a biker rut?" I ask nervously.

"Your tooshie is gonna sting like a bitch when they're through with you. Lucky bitch," Soapbox replies with a sinister chuckle. "I'll get the lube."

"What? No!" I panic.

It takes me several seconds to realize they were just fucking with me, their shit-eating grins giving their game away.

"Uh, you had me there for a second." I chuckle, relieved.

"You should have seen your face. It was like this." Soapbox does an impersonation of me looking terrified, then walks away giggling.

"We're not Neanderthals," Tex mutters, shaking

his head. "But if you ever want to join our sexual escapades, all you've gotta do is ask first."

Everyone disperses around the clubhouse, leaving me with something to think about. The music starts playing. Tex and Rooster set up the pool table. Everything goes back to normal. Bodie and Ivy have finished and are cuddling on the couch beneath a blanket. I can see his hand moving beneath it, stroking her baby bump. This time, seeing is believing. It really does feel like home.

"Uh-oh," Ivy utters with a sudden burst of shock scrawled over her face.

"Baby, did you just pee?" Bodie asks, getting up to swipe his hand against the seat.

Ivy holds her stomach and gasps. "Uh, I think my water just broke."

Everyone rushes around in a moment of panic. Jason shoves the baby bag at Bodie, then Rooster corrals them into his truck to take them to the hospital. All we can do is wait until Bodie calls us with some news. We've still got to tell our parents everything, but I'm too overwhelmed to do it tonight. In a few hours, they'll have a cute bundle of joy to soften the blow.

"Here you go, you've earned it," Tequila says, handing me a shot of clear spirit that I knock back in one fiery gulp. She smacks her lips without so much as a grimace. "I think the prez wants a private word with you," she mentions, her lips curling into a rueful smirk.

Jason snakes his arms around my waist and rests his chin in the crook of my neck. "Do you want to come upstairs and help me shower? I'm not allowed to get my stitches wet."

Rolling my eyes, I give the empty shot glass to Tequila and take Jason's hand as he leads me upstairs. A shower sounds like heaven right now. I could use one to scrub away the filth and shame that I'm forbidden from mentioning again. But before I disappear inside the communal washroom, I spare a lingering look upon the open-plan living space and the family I'd become part of. Jason rests his arm around my shoulders as he joins me, then lovingly kisses the side of my head.

"What are you thinking about, Peaches?"

I twist my lips while I think. "Hmm, this place could surely use a woman's eye. You've been running shit for far too long."

Jason's soft breathy chuckle tickles my ear. "So, what I'm hearing is you're ready to rule at my side?"

My gaze snaps to him, and I wrap my arms around his neck. "Forever and always." I press my lips against his mouth, and we both melt into a deep, sensual kiss.

"Shower and bed," Jason rasps against my lips. "But don't think we'll be sleeping anytime soon. Not until I fuck away every last trace of tonight."

"Mmm, sounds great," I reply with a contented exhale.

Jason slides his warm palm against my cheek, cupping it gently. "You're mine, and only mine. I don't want to share you with anyone. From now on, it's just you and me. I'll never lay my hands on another woman."

I'm so relieved to hear him say that. "And I'll never touch another man."

"I promise, you'll never have to. Never again," Jason vows.

CHAPTER FIFTEEN

Jason peels away his clothing as the shower runs. He covers the taped gauze with a waterproof patch from the hospital, then joins me in the communal shower. It reminds me of the ones they have at the leisure center, but these are not as modern. They're as old as the arc, and the pipes creak and groan whenever the boiler fires up. We're using two out of the six faucets, pressing the buttons every sixty seconds to keep the water flowing. I'm concerned about Bodie bringing a baby into this drafty old steel plant. It's barely sanitary. I don't want child services getting involved when we have a perfectly decent family home they can use. I'll even buy them a new kitchen table because I'm chopping the old one into little pieces and burning it the first chance that I get.

"This isn't permanent," Jason says as if he can read my mind. "This was just a place to lay low until the dust settles. Somewhere to keep off Booker's radar."

I lather a bar of soap between my hands, then set it down on the soap tray. Even that is blistered with rust. "I wonder why Booker didn't come after this place," I reply, sliding my soapy hands over my body. "He went after everywhere else."

Jason smirks. "Oh, believe me. He tried. It was always on his hit list. But you see, this is my land. I inherited it from my grandfather on my mom's side. People always assumed we were dirt poor because of where we used to live, but Gramps hid his wealth from everyone. He was never one to boast," he clarifies, the soap bubbles running down his body as he washes his hair. "It's how I know the land is full of oil." He moves his head beneath the water and scrubs his fingers through his hair to wash out the soap. "Gramps told me before he died."

My jaw drops because of what he said and because I'm watching the soapy water sliding off the end of his pierced monster cock. "Holy shit. You realize this makes you rich, right? You have zero excuse for living like a slob."

Jason rids the water from his eyes and bounces his shoulders in a shrug. "Yeah right, like I could

139

announce it to the world and have vultures like Booker and Marcus flapping around and pecking the meat from my bones? Booker thought my grandfather sold the land to some foreign dude. He's been going around on a wild goose chase looking for the owner for months. I've got big plans for us – for the Hawks – and for Mountview."

"Good for you, babe," I tell him while scrubbing shampoo into my hair.

"Good for us," Jason affirms. "I want to restore all the damage Marcus and his cronies did, then find somewhere permanent for us to settle. Somewhere big enough for all of us to live comfortably without tripping over each other's feet. Then I'll throw some money at the bar, or maybe I'll knock it down and rebuild it." He side-eyes me. "You're right; it's a shit-hole. It's time we cleaned up this town."

We finish showering and brush our teeth, then retire to Jason's bedroom. I feel so clean and refreshed, my skin tingles beneath the heat of the borrowed hairdryer from Claws. Jason takes a call from Dan, and from what I can hear, it all sounds positive. Booker's arrest is breaking news. The reporters are saying the cops have seized all his assets while unraveling his web of corruption. Justice is being served, and it's long overdue. Jason doesn't care that he's named as Mayor

Booker's rape child. All he cares about is his mom and aiding her recovery from her traumatic ordeal. Something puts a genuine smile on Jason's face, and he congratulates Dan and asks if they've set a date. I figure there's going to be wedding bells on the horizon for Liv and Dan, and that's so nice to hear. When Jason ends the call, looking like the weight of the world has been lifted from his shoulders, he plugs the charging cable into his phone and sets it down on the nightstand. I remove the damp towel from my body and toss it on the chair. Jason watches me, dragging his heated gaze all over my body.

"Mom proposed to Dan after all this time," he informs me, confirming what I figured out on my own. His eyes are brimming with happiness. "And he said yes."

I get on the bed and slide beneath the cool sheets. "That's great," I reply, tapping the mattress. "Are you coming to bed?"

Jason plucks at his towel, and it drops to the floor, freeing his pierced appendage. "Do you wanna hear another rule we have?"

"Go on?" I prompt.

Jason goes to the door and opens it fully. "The Hawks leave the bedroom door open to invite people to watch."

My brows almost fly off my forehead with shock. "They do? Oh." This makes me sit up and reflexively cover myself with the bedsheets.

Jason smirks. "Don't worry; they won't interrupt us. There's nothing to be shy about. You've already seen what goes on downstairs and at the Rusty Chain." He comes to the bed and the mattress sinks beneath his weight. "Just focus on us. Nothing else matters." He tucks my hair behind my ear, then kisses me; his hot tongue explores my mouth suggestively, dueling with my tongue, and mimicking what he wants to do to my pussy.

The tip of his iron-hard cock is painting sticky patterns against my hip as we kiss, and the heady scent of arousal fills my lungs, leaving me feeling drunk and light-headed. I want him so badly; it stops me from worrying about who could be watching us from the doorway. I'm so turned on; I'm lukewarm to the idea of being watched. I never thought I would be, but the more Jason touches me, trailing kisses all over my body, then moves around the bed so we're head to tail with each other, I completely forget about the unseen eyes and focus on pleasing my man. The sheets come off. Tossed aside in the need to feel closer, seeking skin-on-skin and the manly heat of his body pressed against mine. I know what he wants as he swings his leg over me and settles his head between my legs, his pierced cock and smooth balls hot and heavy in my face, just begging for some attention.

"I've missed you so much," Jason talks to my pussy right before licking it.

I could say the same thing about his cock. That glorious appendage is a sight for sore eyes compared to Marcus's maggot dick.

It's hard to stay focused while Jason laps at my nerve center, blasting my brains to the moon. So, I concentrate on his cock, dragging my tongue through his pierced cleft, then up and down the smooth shaft, my tongue bumping over the studded Jacob's ladder, circling my fingers around the base of his meat. Then with wet lips, I stretch my mouth around his swollen crown and begin to suck, the awkward angle making me really work for it.

"That feels so good," Jason moans, his hips jerking as I bob my head, his ass cheeks clenching. "I love how you suck my cock. Go deeper. That's it." A ragged moan tears through his throat, and he blasts hot breath against my slick pussy, and as the heat dissipates, it cools my juices. I do as Jason wants, caressing his swollen balls with one hand and fingering the taint of his ass with my opposite hand using my middle finger. Soft, gentle strokes, gliding the pad of my finger around his taut puckered muscle, the contrast of smooth skin and surrounding fine hairs, twitching, and flexing. "Oh, yeah, just like that," Jason encourages me, then continues to lap at my pleasure button, pushing a thick digit inside my pussy and curling it to rub the soft, textured wall of my g-spot. That does it for me. Jason finds my big red detonator button and wastes no time in pressing it.

Our bodies undulate together, slurping, and sucking, our skin getting hotter as we break a sweat. The noises we're making, the grunts and groans of pleasure attract the attention from our friends. I hear their soft footsteps tapping up the stairs, only to halt as they reach the doorway. Not that I see them standing there. My head is angled the wrong way, but I know they can see everything we're doing. Our legs are spread with our heads bobbing against each other's groins, Jason pumping his fingers inside me and uttering dirty words as he feasts on my clit. He can tell by the way my moans turn to desperate cries of ecstasy that I'm cumming hard, which he takes full advantage of, fluttering his tongue over my clit hood until I'm a desperate gasping mess.

"That's it, baby." Jason drags the flat of his tongue through my highly sensitive slit, my pulsing nub jumping at the contact. The mouth of my pussy clenches hard, and Jason's ass bounces above me as he chases his release. "Here it comes." He thrusts his ass, driving his cockhead past my uvula in time for the first hot jet of cum to splat against the back of my throat, feeding me jet after jet of his hot, viscous, salty essence until I wring out the last of it from his balls, gently squeezing to make him squirm with sensitivity.

I almost gag, but it's pure mind over matter that I don't, breathing through my nose and swallowing what I can. I'm proud of my achievement. Jason seems to be too. He drags his cock from my mouth, then crawls around to face me, taking me in his arms while we recover. Not for long though. The Hawks are watching. It's rude to keep them waiting. We touch and kiss until Jason's hard enough to go again. This time, I straddle his hips and work his pierced python inside me, sinking down to the root. He's so big my loins ache from the intrusion. It only eases when I rock my hips to set a steady rhythm. His fat glans slides through my drenched muscles, the stainless-steel body mods hitting the spot with each forward thrust. Jason holds onto my waist and matches the momentum. Movement catches my eye from the doorway, but I don't pay any attention to what they're doing. My focus is on Jason who's slowing down to watch his cock sliding in and out of me, his face scrunched with pleasure, his glistening cock slick with my juices. He leans up to catch my nipple between his teeth, then sucks it into his greedy mouth, the pressure pinching, sending a spark of pain through my breast. Not that it hurts. Quite the opposite. He finds the perfect equilibrium between pleasure and pain to make my pussy flutter around him. I love how we fit and how amazing he feels inside me. Nothing else has ever compared, and nothing ever will.

"Who do you belong to?" Jason asks commandingly, wrapping my hair around his hand and pulling on it just enough to make my head tilt.

"You," I reply, and he tugs a little harder to ignite fire in my scalp.

"That's right," Jason says, his teeth grazing my chin in a playful bite. "You're mine."

He flips us on our side, pulling his cock out of me, then turns me on my front, dragging my hips to force me onto my knees. An almighty smack against my ass makes me shriek unexpectedly. His thumbs pry apart my ass cheeks before he drives his cock back inside me, thrusting hard enough to burst bright lights behind my eyelids.

"This pussy belongs to me," Jason grunts out the words as he forcibly fucks me with abandon, his heavy balls swinging back and forth and slapping against my labia, making lewd wet sounds. "Say it."

"Uh." I struggle to make coherent speech. "It's yours."

The argumentative side of me has taken a backseat. It's his pussy. He'll get no complaints from me.

Jason's fingers dig harder into my hips, his cock-head nestled snugly at my pussy lips. "You're fucking right it is." He plunges inside me, and I cry out as his groin presses flat against my ass again and again until I can't see straight. The bedsprings groan with protest. I think we might break the bed; the headboard is knocking against the wall so hard. "It's mine. You're mine. And I'm gonna claim every inch of you." Perspiration drips from his hair and lands onto my back, his palm sliding through the hot sheen of sweat on my skin, then his thumb rims my asshole. "Rub your clit," he commands me, and I do as he says, licking my finger to ease the glide. "I want you to scream my name when you cum." Warm moisture drips down my ass crack when Jason spits, then my ring of muscle burns as he pushes his thumb inside, my tight star relinquishing control with a silent pop.

My eyes fly open, and I see the figures standing at the door, their shaded eyes watching, and their bodies grinding together with vigorous hand movements against each other's sex organs, letting me know they like what they see. It's so hot. I didn't think I'd like this, and now I'm shocked to learn I love it. Right now, I wouldn't care where we were or who could see. Maybe I'll feel differently when my orgasm wanes and reality crashes me back down to Earth, but somehow I doubt it. Jason drags me to the crest of oblivion and shatters me for the entire crew to see. I cum with a scream, his name tumbling from my lips at an ear-splitting decibel. Jason isn't far behind me. He speeds his momentum, pounding into me like a rutting animal, his cock thickening inside me, fingers pinching my skin, his thumb lodged deep inside my ass. My drenched walls shrink around his pierced, vein-embossed length, feeling every nodule, every ridge, and sending sparks skittering through my loins. I fist the sheets as Jason jerks against me, pumping me full of his hot, viscous cream, then slumping over me breathless and spent.

"I love you, Kiera," Jason utters as he holds me, wrapping me in his hot and sweaty embrace.

The figures at the door retreat, some going into the bedrooms and some going downstairs. Then Tex admonishes Dude for eating all his snacks, but even I know if things are lying around, they belong to the hound.

"I love you too," I reply, turning my head to participate in an awkward kiss.

Jason kisses my shoulder, and I can feel his smile against my skin. "One day, when we can't be accused of stealing anyone's thunder, I'm gonna marry you."

Mrs. Kiera Knight. I like the sound of that.

"Thunder or not, I'm already planning the wedding." I turn to kiss him again.

We cuddle for a while and have one of those deep and meaningful discussions that only lovers share, talking about what we want out of life, and where we want our relationship to go. Jason gets emotional when he talks about his mom, and I know it kills him to think of everything the Jackals did to her. He mentioned wanting to kill all those responsible in a fit of fury, but Dan stopped him from shooting those who surrendered, reasoning with him about seeking retribution the right way. The lawful way. Jason is glad he talked him down because if he'd followed through with it, he'd be no better than Marcus. That's one shit-stain on Jason's family tree he can't wait to eliminate. But despite their cooperation with Mountview Police Department, there's no mention of the Hawks on the news broadcast. It was like they were never there, and that comes as a huge relief to Jason. He and his guys are in the clear.

After a while we decide we can't sleep. So, I wear one of Jason's big T-shirts as a nightdress, and he puts on a pair of sleep shorts, then we join the crew downstairs. Tex turns off the news because it's all about Booker's arrest, and having seen enough of his ugly mug to last us all a lifetime, Tex puts on a music channel instead. I notice the sun coming up through the windows. Hustle orders food, and we're all looking forward to sinking our teeth into breakfast burritos when Bodie calls to announce the birth of my niece, Mylee. Born forty minutes ago. Now all that's left to do is for Bodie to contact our parents and explain his ass off because there's no way in hell that I'm tap dancing onto that minefield. Not in a million years. I've already taken one for the team in more ways than one. Bodie can handle our folks. The cops can handle the douchebags of Mountview. Jason has everything handled here, including me. The only thing left for me to do is to file some paperwork and cash in the insurance policy on the garage. The sooner I get back on the tools, the better. I'm a girl who's not afraid to get her hands dirty. My sexy biker boyfriend can vouch for that.

About the Author

Kelly Lord is a diverse, multi-genre author from England who writes a mixture of contemporary, paranormal, and fantasy romance, both poly and mono, with plenty of action, adventure, and an abundance of steam.

My book links and social media links are on my website: www.kellylord.co.uk

Printed in Great Britain
by Amazon